1453

Constantinople and the Immortal Rulers

Billy Kotsis

1453: Constantinople and the Immortal Rulers
6" × 9" (15.24cm × 22.86cm)
Black & white on white paper

First published September 2020.
First printing print-date.

ISBN-13: 978-1-5136-6589-4

Front cover by Mame Gonzalez Braconi
Book design by Victor Jauregui

Dedicated to every person on the planet who believes in peace. War and violence is no answer, there is no place for hatred on such a small planet. To my own ancestors, from Asia Minor and Lesvos.

Cast

Emperor Constantine Palaiologos

Imperial Secretary & narrator George Sphrantzes

Sultan Mehmed II The Conqueror

Genoan Commander Giovanni Giustiniani

Lord of the Imperial Wardrobe, Chief Byzantine Minister Lukas Notaras

Turkish Prince Orhan

Temporary captain of the sea **Theodora**

The Scot Grant the Scot

Ottoman Commander and Vizier Zaganos Pasha

Grand Vizier Hilal Pasha

Hungarian engineer Orban

Pope Nicholas

Cardinal Isodore

Brothers Bocchiardi

Palace worker **Irene**

Catalan leader Don Francisco de Toledo

Leaders of the Cretans **Captain Michalis**

Admiral Baltoghlu

Harbourmaster **Persephone**

Fierce warrior Hasan

Actress/Thespian **Despoina**

Venetian Captain in the Horn Coco

Helena mother of the emperor

Innocent bystanders the people of Constantinople and Thrace

Acknowledgments

Proof-readers Shirley Kaptanos Katsoulakos, thanks for all your suggestions too, and Michael as well, both appreciated, Sophie Papatheocharous in Cyprus, thanks heaps and for doing this during your well-earned break and Gina Mamouzelos, a Greek-Australian journalist who is a great supporter of some of my work, efharisto.

Ana Cordeiro Director and writer of the two love scenes from Brasil. Obrigado.

Cover design Mame Gonzalez Braconi, in Argentina. Always makes any cover design look brilliant.

Drawings CC Graphics na'se kala. Two wonderful people, and one who is good at discussing great issues, the other a talented singer.

Book design/typography Victor Jauregui from the fields of Santiago Bernabéu

Background

I wrote this book because I never made the film. The film I wanted to make, was a screenplay I commenced in 2006. Took it with me to London two years later with the intention of writing it properly. It was called *1453*.

My laptop crashed in my Crystal Palace flat, and with it the sections and characters I had developed. Soon, I learnt that London was good for travelling extensively, meeting people and enjoying the culture and parties; and writing a very occasional article, rather than a screenplay. Despite all that, I still scouted some locations for the *film* in Greece and Africa and kept the idea going over an ouzo or two with some of my friends.

In 2012, a Turkish film made it to the cinema. It raked in an impressive 100 million dollars at the box office, becoming the highest grossing Turkish film of all time. A lot of the acting was wooden. One night, I gathered my film buff friends to watch it with me; they abandoned me early on during the screening as it just did not pull them in. It demonstrated that the film probably only appealed to certain groups and could do with a touch of Hollywood, or in my case, BillyWood.

In 2020, Netflix produced a decent Ottoman docudrama series that again may have only appealed to certain groups. The previous year, I had decided to write 1453 as a book rather than attempt a film. The idea is to provide a better perspective and insight into the defenders, which the 2012 film did not achieve.

There are significant first-person accounts of the siege from Greeks and Italians; they are the sources I initially followed before listening to the accounts from Turks, English and Serbs as I needed some balance.

You will note, this book is not anti-Turk. If you are a Greek nationalist reading, best to stop now. Similarly, if you are a Turkish nationalist, stop reading as well. Patriots, however, on both sides are welcome and I always enjoy listening to viewpoints. This is a book taking elements of fact and history and meshing it with elements of fiction and fantasy to allow you to understand what was happening during the siege and in the lead up. I have done this in a measured way. Its why you will see some flashbacks to other eras of Byzantine history to give you the context of the empire; and the mess of the empire by 1453.

Occasionally, I praise the sultan and at the same time underline how ruthless he was. You cannot sugar coat his ruthless elements such as the ransacking of Constantinople, executing messengers or prisoners and almost killing his own loyal admiral who was up against the superior Italian and Greek navy.

I explain elsewhere that this is not a Greek vs Turkish siege. The Greeks were joined by a range of fighters from abroad, some Muslim. For the attackers, it is difficult to imagine that pure multigenerational Turks who fought for the sultan were in the overwhelming majority. It was a multiethnic empire with a short history to that point.

On the Byzantine side, you will find Genoans, Venetians, Turks, Catalans, possibly some Pisans and other Christians including Serbs who fled from the sultan, along with the Greeks and one Scotsman.

The sultan had Turks, the fearsome Janissaries who were born Christian, Germans, a Hungarian, Serbs, other Christians including Greeks, non-Turkish Muslims and 'barbarians.'

It is not even an Asia vs Europe fight; both empires had straddled the two continents, and each one maintained their capital in Europe.

This is the last battle/war of the medieval ages and represents the beginning of modern times. The advance of weapons and the changing of the guard of one great empire for another was indeed the start of modern history. The changing of the guard process had been in train since the 1350s when the Ottomans made it to

Europe.

You will also find throughout this account, the inability of Europe to come to the aid of Constantinople. Religious differences played a huge part in not offering better support, jealousy of the Greeks and various inter European feuds such as the Hundred Years War. The Ottoman Empire was very powerful by this stage; a concerted support of Byzantium would have seen Constantinople saved. This is not an 'if', as the city would have been saved. How long it would have remained with the Byzantines thereafter? That is the question! Maybe a few decades, a century. It would have fallen at some stage in early modern history to the Ottomans as the Spanish, Portuguese, French and English looked to the Atlantic and Africa to ruthlessly exploit. Russia was not yet powerful and central Europe was not keen on adventures near Asia. Why swap the bitter cold for better climate?

As for the Italian republics, they would have been possible allies if they had united, though generally they preferred commerce and taking small ports and islands, which were much easier to bully into submission. Ironically, these were mostly Greek speaking territories.

In terms of belligerents, I have tried to be as true to the numbers as I can. Some estimates placed the Ottoman forces significantly higher than mine. I have used figures which most likely seem based on a range of sources I have researched since I was at school.

Another point to be mindful of, Byzantines were *Roman.* They always called themselves that, despite speaking Greek, having a separate religion to the Vatican as the centuries progressed and Rome as a city only playing a small role in the long history of the Byzantine. Modern scholars actually called the East Roman Empire the *Byzantine* due to the original name of Constantinople being Byzantium. They were never known as Byzantines until recent centuries when historians coined the term.

By and large since the end of the 500s AD, when Greek replaced Latin in the bureaucracy to keep up with Greek as the common language, it was a Greek meets a multi-ethnic empire, with emperors being a mix of Greek, Armenian, Latin and even part Serbian (Constantine Palaiologos certainly thanks to Helena). By the 900s and beyond, it really is a Greek empire in all but name as territory no longer stretched deep into Latin lands.

I hope this book enables you to learn more about this great city and why it was desired by rulers from Europe and Asia.

Read me—style of the book

Some of the main protagonists in the book use 'first person' as I want them to have a direct conversation with you. At other times, Sphrantzes does the narration and then, of course, you will note normal discussions between some of the people/characters.

Across the chapters, you will also find some elements of humour in the way the story is told, for not every action and person involved needs to be dramatic. The battles themselves and the mood of the Constantinople will provide plenty of drama.

Most of what I have written is based on facts. Some of it has a creative license. For example, we do not know enough about Grant and he was certainly not a 'bookie;' hence, I have provided a back story on what he was doing in the Constantinople by leading the countermining operations. With the key Greek, Italian and Ottoman participants, I try to keep to the facts. As I want you to see this as somewhat of a movie, there is the stretching of the deeds of heroes; there was never a competition by the emperor, Giustiniani and the Bocchiardi brothers to lead sorties against the enemy, though this was the domain of the brothers.

Stories of the female characters, are by use of a creative license. That is an element that appears to be missing from the last years of Byzantium, the role of women who are unrepresented in most accounts of the siege. I did not want women to be invisible, which seems to be the trend for most of the medieval era. Helena of course is real; the other women and their contributions are not. In the list of characters/cast above, those in bold did not exist. Ditto the visit of Sphrantzes to Venice at any time before the siege, it is likely he was there by 1455 as the ambassador for the Morea. Not before.

We know that the Cretans were in Constantinople and fought tooth and nail. They never surrendered, true to their toughness. Mehmed allowed them to leave thanks to their gallantry. Again, I created a backstory for why they were and their leader, who is named after a Nikos Kazantzakis character, Captain Michalis, in Freedom or Death, who was likely created in honour of his dad! This is my tribute to this brilliant, progressive Cretan writer who told us the story of an uprising against the Turks.

For the purposes of simplifying the Ottoman generals, I have condensed them to be the 'commanders' and Zaganos Pasha.

The siege occurred from 6 April until 29 May and it includes an *alternative ending* which adjusts the ending slightly from the previous chapter. You will note there is a general timeline with several flashbacks, as I want you to understand a little more about Byzantium.

When you have read the novel, come back and read this section. I hope the book piques your interest to explore Byzantium and this great siege. Both leaders were people that deserve the respect of all of us. Both were brave, visionary and at times cruel, a product of their time and positions. I do not condone any of their (or subordinates') actions that led to the death, murder, slavery, rape of innocent people. Today, we have the Geneva Convention in place, but what good does it do for many people around the world, who remain occupied by other countries, or people who remain in slavery?

The City

From the outset, I would like to ask you, the reader, for your opinion. Can you tell me what the most significant cities of all time are? Can you tell me what would be the greatest city of Greek history?

I'm sure opinions would be varied and can be debated for hours. When I ask my friends and colleagues, they usually answer the former question with the following cities: Alexandria, Jerusalem, Rome, Carthage, Athens, Babylon, New York, Tokyo and of course Rio de Janeiro, (hey they like Brasil). My friends and colleagues would answer the latter question with the following cities: Athens, Sparta, Corinth, Thessaloniki, Alexandria, Thebes, Syracuse, Mytilene (o.k. I'm the only one who includes my hometown).

There is however another city that rivals all of these places, one of the greatest of all time. This is a city that has existed for thousands of years and has been the scene of many of history's most significant moments. The home of one of the greatest empires in history, the home of two world religions, a city of two continents and two seas and a place where many stories are told and will be told.

This is a city that has seen more twists and turns than any literary novel. I will keep you guessing as to its identity for a little while longer, but I will give you a hint, it was named after an emperor and today whilst no longer being Greek, it still has a Greek name.

In 1453, the world witnessed one of the greatest and most heroic sieges. The well-organised and superior military machine of the Ottoman Empire took aim at one of the last independent cities of the Byzantine Empire (Medieval Greek). It is often said that when the great canons of the Ottomans' Hungarian engineer, Orban, began blasting the city's great walls on 6 April, it was the end of the Middle Ages and the beginning of modern times.

The city I have been alluding to is the city of Constantine, CONSTANTINOPLE. It was founded by the Greeks of Megara in 657 BC and became an important trading colony and link between the city-states and kingdoms of Greece and the new settlements in the Black Sea.

In 324 AD, the Roman Emperor Constantine made the momentous decision of renaming the city after himself and moving the Empire's capital to "Constantinople." Over the next few decades, the city grew in importance, and as the Roman Empire crumbled with Rome itself being overrun by barbarians, Constantinople soon became the capital of what was to be known as the Byzantine Empire, the Greek empire of the medieval times.

The Empire at its peak would rule over almost the entire Mediterranean, including southern Spain in the east, Syria and Persia in the west, North Africa in the south and the Balkans in the north. The peak came through conquests in the sixth century and again in the eleventh century. Other than those centuries, the Empire ruled over what was called the Greek world, places that included southern Italy, the Black Sea, Asia Minor, the Balkans, Alexandria and of course Constantinople. The common language was Greek and by the 600s, Latin was removed from the bureaucracy. Citizens did however call themselves Roman, as the notion of being a 'Greek' disappeared for many centuries. I have been to places in the Ukraine where people still speak the old Greek language and call themselves "Romai." I will never forget the first time I heard this term; I was in the village of Sartana in the Ukraine and a woman said to me, "we are the Romai." It sent a chill through my entire body.

How do you explain to people that Byzantium, a term for the 1,100-year history of the Empire, is full of rich cultural, religious, artistic, literary and scientific achievements?

Achievements include the formulation of a new language for

Slavic peoples who appeared in the Balkans in the sixth century AD. The Cyrillic alphabet was devised by Greek speaking brothers Cyril and Methodius. Christianity flourished and was spread across the empire, Byzantine architecture was, in a word, triumphant. Public buildings were of the highest order, Byzantine mosaics and frescoes were captivating, and art and literature had a profound impact on civilisation. For example, the Renaissance had its foundations set in the works of the Greeks of Byzantium. Today, you can still see some of the Byzantine achievements in Italy, notably in Venice, Ravenna, Calabria, Apulia, Tunisia, Jerusalem, Syria, Alexandria, Turkey and the Balkans, not to mention in Greece.

Throughout history, Constantinople was the envy of the world. It was a cultural and economic phenomenon. At one stage there were 500,000 people residing in Constantinople, with the overwhelming percentage being of Greek descent. However, there were people of all ethnicities that resided or traded in the city, including Arabs, Persians, Spaniards, Venetians and other Italians, Franks, Ukrainians, Russians, Germans and the list goes on. When the great siege took place in 1453, all of these nationalities played a role in the story of the siege.

In the two centuries leading up to the fall of Constantinople, the empire had seen a series of catastrophes. A plague, which wiped out half of the population, a number of Greek civil wars (typically, a Greek history lesson can never be complete unless there is civil war and intrigue), various sieges and the Latin states' betrayal and capture of Constantinople for 60 years. It is this last point which had a lasting impact on Greeks and the history of Constantinople. The Latins not only massacred Greeks in the city, which was a reprisal for the Greek attacks in the previous century, they brought about the decline of the Byzantine economy and stole countless treasures from the city. In fact the two great horses in Saint Mark's Square in Venice were brought there by the Latins in the 1200s (the church of Saint Mark was originally built by the

Byzantines).

By the time the Greeks, led by Michael VIII Palaiologos, had recaptured their capital of Constantinople in 1261, it was a shadow of its former great self, though it still produced a great number of artists and leaders over the next 200 years. It was still richer than most downtrodden European cities.

Medieval times, just like the ancient, were full of wars and siege warfare. Constantinople had been under siege many times before from the Latins, Russians, Crusaders, Ottomans, Persians, Arabs, Avars, Slavs, Bulgarians.

This book, hopefully, highlights the role of two brilliant leaders on opposite sides and two significant empires, each leaving a legacy and a mark on the world. It is not simply a Greek vs Turkish story; it really is two empires and two brilliant leaders with their allies of different religions fighting for a grand prize. For the sultan, Constantinople would be the fulfilment of a Muslim prophecy and the ultimate prize for his empire.

Contents

1	I am George Sphrantzes	1
2	A quick battle in Thrace, 1453	5
3	Palaiologoi	11
4	Troops of the Sultan arrive	17
5	Flashback to the younger sultan	23
6	January arrival of Giustiniani	29
7	The deeds of Giustiniani flashback	35
8	Emperor and Theodora	43
9	Flight to Trebizond	47
10	Grant the Scot	51
11	Emperor and the defences	55
12	Another Flashback: Grant and his companion	57
13	Cretans have landed	61
14	Arrival	65
15	Orban's cannon	71
16	Venice, the pope, some Russians and a cardinal	73

17	Heraclius and Basil Flashback	79
18	A tough attack	83
19	The attack of the Serbians	91
20	From Prince Orhan to the engineer Orban	93
21	Better the turban . . .	97
22	Baltoghlu on dangerous seas	101
23	Another way to attack	107
24	Quarrel, Italian style	111
25	Return from Trebizond	117
26	Genoese boat returns from Aegean	121
27	Tunnel Vision	123
28	A good time to be a miner	127
29	Ottoman boats slip in	133
30	Counterattack Failure	137
31	A Scottish Tragedy	143
32	Immortal Emperor, 28th May	147
33	Can't win with the sword, pray instead	155
34	Decider	161
35	Cretans refuse to surrender	177
36	Theodora	183
37	Alternative ending . . .	187
38	Postscript	205

Chapter 1

I am George Sphrantzes, loyal secretary, diplomat and occasional narrator

Let me tell you something about me, something about my emperor and perhaps a few home truths. I am the secretary for the emperor and his confidant. I am the bearer of reality and sobering news. There is not much to smile about in my life this period.

It may have been better not to have been born into this life at all.[1]

What had been the point? Our great empire had been reduced to fragments, with enemies from all sides and all comers. Our Christian brothers and sisters, the infidel from Asia, the Crusaders, Slavs, Bulgars, fortune seekers. The list was endless. All of these ungratefuls had gained from us. Be it a religion, a language for the Slavs and Bulgars, holding out eastern invaders, architecture, governance or marrying some of our princesses.

What had we done wrong to deserve the vultures? It would

[1]Written by Sphrantzes in his memoir after the fall of Constantinople.

have been better if they were eagles rather than vultures, which are a vulgar species and prone to disease carrying unlike the stylish eagles.

Indeed, the vultures were circling. Sometimes, sometimes, those same vultures end up with vertigo.

In 1402, Timur the Mongol had annihilated the forces of the sultan, inadvertently buying us time. Pesky Serbs, Bulgarian, Hungarian warriors and the last remaining Greek outposts of the Balkans were providing a buffer for Constantinople. Our emperor toured Europe including England for help, which was met with sympathy and bad teeth.

However, ever since the sultan illegally created the Throat Cutter two years ago on the Bosporus, we have known that time is no longer with us. Not because none of us have a time piece or sun dial, it is just that the Ottomans are coming.

In March, my emperor bade me to ascertain the count of fighting men in Constantinople. Additionally, I was to count weapons and resources to sustain a siege. I always undertake the important tasks for the emperor.

Over the course of a day I made my way through the dry markets, the Venetian quarter and across every church and imperial building, occupied or not. The figures were depressing.

I may have been tardy in mentioning that I was an attendant with Constantine's father in the royal court since I was a teenager and followed the prince to the Morea in 1427. There he set me up as governor of Glarentza, the port town facing the Adriatic, whilst he was based at Mystra.

Over the course of our years together, I helped arrange his marriages, including his second to Caterina Gattilusio, princess of Lesvos in 1440.

I had been on Lesvos in December of that year and returned a few months later with the prince and Lukas Notaras, aptly titled Chief of the Imperial Wardrobe, mega doux of the imperial navy and chief minister. He certainly had titles! Despite the decline of the wealth of the empire, the wedding was moderately lavish, with banquets and gold cutlery, traditional musicians and a who's who of Lesvos and Genoa. Both the bride and groom were an easy match with their dark features and natural warmth. She was beautiful and he was handsome, bearded and charismatic with a good grasp of romance!

The locals served some unique alcohol which was produced in their small port of Plomari. I can still feel it on my tastebuds to this day. I never knew what it was called. It certainly oozed a delightful taste.

Constantine spent almost a year on the island. He used the time to practise fighting techniques and attend to imperial business from Mytilene, the capital of the island. We returned to the Morea in 1441 without Caterina and then returned a year later to pick Caterina up for his return to Constantinople. We had a detour to Lemnos, where a skirmish took place from an Ottoman fleet that was passing by. They were no match for our superior sailors and soon moved on. We possessed the skilled sailors and Greek fire, against a fledgling navy.

This detour and delay came at an inopportune time as Caterina, who was pregnant, caught a local virus. A miscarriage occurred before our departure to Constantinople, from the virus, and she passed away a few months later in the imperial palace on Lemnos. The emperor initially struggled with this loss. He seemed down for many months, as any good husband and father-to-be would in those circumstances. He soon adapted, knowing that the empire was his family, one that he could love and protect.

⋆⋆

This is the norm in my life and relationship with Constantine. In better times, I acted as his ambassador and helped him retake territory in the Morea and central Greece including Athens. He also brought me home, twice, after having being kidnapped. Pirates in the Ionian Sea had kidnapped me as I was making my way to Epiros. I am grateful that Constantine paid the ransom rather than letting me be eaten by these damn pirates.

Another time, in 1429 near Patras, my troops and I were captured after a small battle with Venetian forces. Constantine gathered together a force of 300 from Mystra, which is close to Sparta in Laconia. Constantine speedily rode out to Patras within a few moons. During a night offensive, Constantine personally led the men into the well-guarded fortress and brutally suppressed all the defenders. To see the prince in his purple regalia atop his mount slashing at well trained soldiers after a frenetic ride, tells you the type of soldier he is. On the battlefield, there is no one more ruthless as the fallen bodies could testify. Constantine, true to his benign nature however, released all prisoners on the proviso that they leave Greece. "You tell foreigners that you meet of the clemency of the empire, my ruthlessness in battle and the will of God," was all he asked in return.

This is my bond and friendship with Constantine. The emperor. I am also his chronicler and drinking buddy, along with Notaras. The Catalans called us the three amigos. They were not wrong.

Chapter 2

A quick battle in Thrace, 1453

It is never a good idea.... An idea with possible good outcomes, can be a good idea. An idea to venture into Thrace away from the walls of Constantinople is not a good idea when the Ottomans are in full flight. We still controlled hundreds of square kilometres in Thrace; from the Aegean to the Sea of Marmara, the Bosporus and the Black Sea. Sounds impressive, though if you look at the map, it really is a medium size area. There lived tens of thousands of our people in these boundaries. Outside of our borders, the Turks had gained European territory at our expense and were fast encroaching upon what remained of our lands. We protested to the sultan. We complained to the Pope. We prayed to our God. If only there was a *League of Empires* we could complain to or a *United Kingdom's* group. Sadly, we were on our own.

By April, town after town on the path toward the city was being razed and looted. Thousands perished. Many fled to the city or found safe passage to Venice or the Greek islands.

The emperor had had enough. We tried to convince him to

leave Constantinople for exile and safety. Constantine would not be deterred. On the 25th March he rode out with a small force of warriors, including the mighty Varangian Guard, a few of the Catalan mercenaries, and Greeks.

A note on the Guard. This was once the elite force or crack mercenaries that were loyal to the emperor only. Their life commenced five centuries ago; most have been drawn from Anglo-Saxon countries and also the Rus. They were that prestigious and popular, that in Sweden, a law was passed prohibiting those who joined the Guard from owning land in Sweden upon their return. It was designed to halt Swedes from joining. This was known as the Greece law. Sadly, in the last few decades as the financial reward decreased and the expeditions outside the walls of Constantinople came to a halt, this crack group almost disappeared. The few remaining Guard members are now Greek or from lands connecting Kiev and Moscow. *The very few I should emphasise.*

⋆⋆

Always known for his lightning speed, the emperor raced ahead at a crazy pace through mountain ridges and lush green forests, with rivers flowing endlessly through them. The double headed eagle on his gold standard would not have kept up on this day.

The group reached the town of Arcadiopolis, which was already up in flames. The barbarians, probably a posse of 60 were startled since they were not expecting to see riders from Constantinople.

The town which had been home to several hundred people lay in ruins, with a handful of men and women attempting to hold off the barbarians.

"Greek dogs," came a cry from some of the barbarians.

"Turkish dogs," came the taunt from the Varangian Guard. They had proven to be, as always, loyal to emperors of Constantinople and today was to be no exception. The sultan's troops were quickly surrounded and after a quick resistance, they lay down their arms.

Running from behind an overturned cart, a well-dressed woman ran to the leader of the sultan's troops who had placed his hands on his head, who was feigning defeat. He was ready to leap up at any time to wrestle the soldier in front of him. However, he was no match for the wits of the woman and what she witnessed earlier as she plunged a dagger into the leader's heart, if he did have a heart.

"Dog, skilo," she yelled as he buckled over in a pool of blood.

The emperor immediately jumped off his mount and grabbed the dagger from her manicured hand.

"Theodora, enough death for one day." The emperor gently whispered to her. "I am just glad you are fine." He embraced his mistress.

Theodora had become his companion since returning from Mystra four years ago. The younger cousin of his friend Lukas Notaras. The two embraced and shared a passionate kiss in front of the soldiers.

Some of the men laughed at this wanton behaviour and others asked the emperor why he only ever kissed them on the cheeks!

Looking around the town, there were only a few survivors. Many had been killed and others had fled. The captives were chained and taken back to the capital with an escort from the Catalans, with some of the survivors from the town.

"We heard earlier that the enemy had taken many towns and villages, and a fortress on the Bosporus and the castle at Studius." Theodora said in an angry and pensive manner. It was quite possible that steam was pouring out of her ears. Her dress straining under her heaving bosom.

"It is true, my scouts have confirmed the losses. They have taken several small settlements toward Adrianople that belong to the empire and who knows how many villages." The emperor responded with a sigh.

The black-haired Theodora mounted her horse, a glorious white haired and black bodied animal.

"Come on, we have the next town ahead to save. Pame, figame (let's go)."

With no argument from the emperor, the remaining soldiers sped off to the next town, which was perched on a hill. Again, smoke.

A peculiar skinny, bald, pasty white ginger bearded engineer spoke to the emperor.

"As you know, my eyesight is as good as that eagle on your banner. I can make out no more than 50. They are bunched up, appears as though hand to hand combat is taking place. The villagers have no protective armour just a few swords and the spirit of your God."

"How your eyesight can adjust from tunnels to daylight never ceases to amaze me Grant. This is what we will do. Varangian leader take your troops around the bend in the hill, there is a pathway ahead. Greeks and Scotsman Grant, you are coming with me for a full-frontal assault. Hurry, we can still save the people."

The attack played out as the emperor had expected. The Varangian Guard who are ruthless made it to the town first and with no emperor to temper their temper, ruthlessly cut down the enemy. The size of the Ukrainians in the Guard, almost at giant proportions, with hulking muscle and frame, with the speed and agility to match are unmatched by simple Ottoman soldiers.

As the Greeks arrived with Sphrantzes and Theodora, carrying their paramerion, saber-style blades that cavalry would carry on their belts, to mop up the tail, the emperor had no need to call it off as none of the enemy wanted to surrender this time. They choose to fight for honour. One by one they were taken down.

The troops embraced the few dozen townspeople who had stayed to fight. Under normal circumstances, music would be played, and food eaten. It would normally be a joyous occasion for the emperor to appear. On this sombre night, the tired people and warriors eased into sleep, except the emperor, Theodora and Sphrantzes, along with well-positioned sentries and lookouts.

Sphrantzes and the Scottish engineer took a reconnaissance mission and reported back.

“The main army is a day’s march from us. It is best that we return to the city tomorrow at first light. I Stin Poli, my emperor.”

The emperor agreed to the intelligence. One of the few leaders of a word power who genuinely listened to intelligence and advice.

At daybreak, soldiers dressed and prepared for the day ahead, taking any supplies that they could find from the town.

On the way back to Constantinople, the emperor took the troops on two detours to liberate two small settlements that were also being harassed by small numbers of the enemy. Easily defeating their opponents yet again, the emperor now turned his attention to the defences of the city, and his beautiful brunette Goddess.

Chapter 3

Palaiologoi and a visit to the Morea (Peloponnese)

Let me interrupt my secretary, to tell you about me. My name is Constantine Dragases Palaiologos; I am possibly the last in the line of a long empire. I am also known as the representative of God on earth, and my official title is *Autocrat* of the people, Basileus kai autokratōr Rhomaiōn. You will find the symbol of my family is a double headed eagle which has been used extensively by a plethora of cultures, this includes Christian and Muslim; I am not sure who truly owns the 'copyright.' I believe the origins are from Mycenean Greece or Asia Minor. According to Sphrantzes, the symbol made its way to the court of Constantinople under emperor Isaac I Komnenos four centuries in the past when the empire was in a very strong position, though there had been a recent civil war. We cannot seem to extricate ourselves from moments of civil war when we should be fighting barbarians.

My father is a Greek and my mother is the Serbian Helena, hence I also use her family name Dragases to honour her and how she was always supportive of me. I have a feeling I was her

Figure 3.1: In Mystras, statue of the emperor. Image courtesy of Nick Kom.

favourite. She is special too, then again, every mother is for every Greek or Serbian man!

Speaking of family, two centuries ago, my ancestors regained Constantinople from the barbaric, unruly, temporary rulers of my city. The Latins had been a nuisance during their temporary rule of the city of my birth for a number of decades two centuries prior. On paper, the restored East Roman Empire of 1261 appeared as a strong political entity with boundaries that took in 35% of Asia Minor, the southern Balkans, some of the Aegean islands and a tributary state in Epiros. My ancestors therefore held an empire stretching from the Adriatic to the Black Sea, and the Aegean to the Mediterranean. It was soon undermined by civil wars and the expansion of the Ottoman Empire, along with mistrust of the Pope and Venice whose growth came at the expense of Constantinople. The commercial growth of Venice and the decline of my Constantinople ensured that the empire was not economically viable. The Venetians had too many trade concessions in Constantinople and their fleet was the biggest in the world.

We could have halted the Ottomans at the gates of Europe. Alas, the Ottomans landed troops and secured Gallipoli in 1351, as our people fought another civil war between royal rivals. This was the last chance to keep us as a preeminent power in Europe. The last. Rather than concern themselves with foreigners, my ancestors did what seemed to come natural to them: fight a civil war!

Constantinople declined even further. There had been half a million people living there at its peak in the Sixth Century AD, there were perhaps 60,000 at this stage. Impressive for a medieval city, however, not for the once world superpower as we had been.

As a counterbalance, an incredible situation emerged in the Peloponnese. The home of Corinth, Sparta, Argos and Patras, was now flourishing. At the Battle of Pelagonia, my ancestors won against the Latin/Frankish forces in 1259. With this victory we regained most of the Morea which was known as the Peloponnese in the times of Thucydides.

The Morea became known as a place for learning, philosophy, the arts and the classics. We nurtured cities such as Monemvasia and Mystra (near Sparta) which grew in stature with impressive buildings and castles.

Emperor, John VI Kantakouzenos, allowed his son Manuel Kantakouzenos to rule in the Morea from 1359. In 1383 Theodore Palaiologos became Despot of the Morea, though it was still very much part of the Empire. Theodore recognised the Ottomans and may have paid a tributary; he also encouraged Albanian migration to help boost the economy via cheap labour.

By 1430, the entire Morea was under our control; 'our' being my brothers, Demetrios, Thomas and myself, of the Palaiologos clan.

I captured cities such as Patras and built the Hexamilion (six mile) Wall along the Isthmus at Corinth, before moving into central Greece with my loyal troops and fighting with whoever was an enemy of Constantinople. We recaptured Athens and Thebes by 1444.

Murad II, the father of the current sultan, Mehmed, attacked the Hexamilion and destroyed it in December 1446. I was lucky to get away. Sixty thousand people of the Morea were taken prisoner and sold to slavery in Asia Minor. Our resources were stretched despite our fighting abilities as we faced an enemy five times larger than ours. Yes, we may have inflicted at least double the fatalities of the enemy, yet you cannot beat an endless supply of men. Just ask Pyrrhus, he would tell you.

In 1448, when my brother Manuel passed away in Constantinople, I was subsequently crowned emperor in Mystra. This was an unusual coronation as it was held far from home. I had to do it, otherwise one of my surviving brothers would have made the attempt to be crowned emperor. The crown jewels were almost worthless, and I had to beg a ride on a Genoan warship to take me to my Constantinople.

⋆⋆

George Sphrantzes, my secretary, always says, what could have been if I had been born in another era. Our first emperor was a Constantine. A prophecy has said that the last will also be a Constantine. Fortunately, I have a second name, Dragases and I have no intention of being the last ruler. None.

Look out for me on the battlefield, I like to lead the men with purple imperial regalia, and I love my horse. She reminds me of Bucephalus; together we are almost invincible.

These last years have been an interesting time for me, for it included some losses that were difficult to absorb. Losses appear to be a theme. I lost both of my wives to mysterious illnesses, one died in childbirth. Tragic. I can't say I was happy to lose the Hexamilion.

At Varna that same year, Hunyadi and his Hungarians were roundly defeated by the Ottomans. Another loss. These are our natural allies, and I use the word natural as we share a common a God. Yet most of our allies in the West have failed us in recent times. The struggles of Emperor Alexios in the eleventh century with pillaging and disrespectful crusaders ravaging our lands. Then a Latin betrayal a few decades later as a 'crusade' under the Venetian Doge, took the city with treachery. Pathetic betrayal. After that, the empire splintered into three small Greek empires that fought the Latins and then each other. Now we have had to proclaim a union with the Pope as we fear what is coming from the sultan.

We betray our own Church to protect our empire. The people are not overly enthused with the union. In fact, many in the city will tell you, "it's better the turban of the sultan, rather than the hat of the Papa." Ironic, for many of the early popes were Greek.

I have appealed to the pope for troops. For resources. Money. Men. Equipment. Boats. I wrote my request and heard little in return. Perhaps it is all Greek to him! My predecessor, who was my brother also made the same appeals to the Papal region and beyond, with only lip service as the response.

Chapter 4

Troops of the Sultan arrive

October in the Morea can be just another day in summer. Calm, blue waters on the coastline, the impressive and lush greenery of many forests, the occasional sizzling hot day and wildlife in abundance including a number of single headed eagles.

It had been three years since their brother Constantine had been proclaimed Basileus in Mystra. He was not the eldest, he was simply the ablest. Both Thomas and Demetrios did *harbor* some resentment. On a day when both were in the harbour of Monemvasia with a fleet of 20 boats, men, icons and supplies, more eagles came circling above. Neither of the brothers had quite figured what the eagles' significance was, when they were called abruptly from the scoutmaster.

The harbourmaster wasn't your ordinary harbourmaster. Her name was Persephone. A name from the glorious times of the ancient Greeks, she had continued a recent tradition of Greek speaking women in the Peloponnese being more visible. It had become a necessity, especially after the collapse of the Hexamilion and 60,000 mostly males being sent to slavery just a few years earlier. *Efharisto Constantine and Sphrantzes! Merhaba Murad!*

Persephone came running down to the two despots. Her hair willowing in the wind.

"Sirs, sirs, we have a problem, the Turkoi are a few kilometres away with a fleet of about 40 ships."

The brothers looked at each other and jumped on their respective saddles and rode out with the harbourmaster to the tower beyond the harbour. As the eagles followed above, the trio dismounted at the tower and climbed 90 stoned steps to the top.

Demetrios looked at Thomas, before they both looked at the fleet. Was it worth throwing away their own little fiefdom just to help their brother on a suicide mission?

"Persephone, I want you to send out a negotiating team with a few bars of gold. We will happily avert war or a visit to the city if they do not attack. We still remember the tragic result of the Hexamilion. Safety comes first and foremost."

A mystified, pale Persephone could only nod, turning away. A teardrop rolled down her cheek to the ground.

⋆⋆

Some weeks earlier, a standard bearer for the emperor rode to the edge of the empire in Asia, facing Syria with Manzikert to his rear; he proclaimed:

"A new campaign season is being called. The sultan, our leader and son of Murad, is asking for all able men to join the sultan in six months' time at Adrianople to fight the infidel. There will be riches and rewards as we fight for our honour. We need fighters, soldiers, engineers, cooks, tailors, cloth spinners, carpenters, masons, blacksmiths and any trade that can help us prepare for battle against Rum."

This, the standard bearer repeated in almost hundreds of towns until his voice became hoarse and his horse gave way. Tens of thousands heeded the call and subsequently made their way to

Edirne. Some knew the city as Adrianople as they had been converts in recent years or recent generations, remembering the names of the former Greek towns of their ancestors.

Men of muscle and strength were joined by fortune seekers, thrill seekers, men with violent streaks (a welcome respite for their immediate friends and villages), religious fanatics and even those who felt some sort of injustice from an enemy that had long been absent from Anatolia.

By the time January and the snow made its way to the European part of the empire, as did 70,000 soldiers and fighters. The sultan ensured caravans, carts and boats were made available to transport the would-be soldiers to Europe. They were joined by non-fighters of various skills. This included women who would be part of more unsavoury acts to keep the men calm during a long siege. Not much had changed in thousands of years of fighting when it came to the behaviour of males. And as long as the oldest profession in the world existed and was tolerated, then all parties would *benefit*. This unsavoury element may have been called *parties with benefits*, then again, what do I know?

Across the over 70,000 fighters, one could see a split into three categories. The first being unskilled and untrained 'fighters' who thought this would be a quick and easy fight, regular soldiers drawn from across the provinces and the Janissaries. The formidable and disciplined Janissaries.

They were joined by several thousand troops from 'tributary ally' Stephan Ducan of Serbia. None of these men wanted to be there. As a tributary ally, they could join the fight or risk the sultan destroying Serbia. The memory of the devasting loss at Kosovo was still fresh in the Serbian psyche.

Next up came in excess of 40,000 soldiers from the European provinces. Soldiers with recent experience fighting Constantine in the Morea as well as other victories in the Balkans including Varna nine years before.

Along with the personal fighting force of the sultan, and volunteers who came from outside the empire, a military machine of almost 120,000 land forces had been brought together. Notwithstanding the navy forces, the Ottoman forces were a huge and scary sight. Even a blind man would be unable to see how the Sultan had the upper hand. And probably the lower hand too.

By March, these forces had been readied and drilled in siege warfare and expectation. It was time to prepare for the march toward the ultimate prize. All the participants in the campaign were acutely aware that despite their service to the sultan, it was the possibility of three days of unhindered looting that would inspire a real prize. For others, there was a religious angle, as it had once been a prophecy that the city would fall to them, and they genuinely wanted involvement should the city fall.

⋆⋆

The sultan gave a rousing speech to his assembled soldiers in March. "My friends and men of my empire! You all know very well that our forefathers secured this kingdom that we now hold. It was gained at the cost of many struggles and very great dangers and that, having passed it along in succession from their fathers, from father to son, they handed it down to me. For some of the oldest of you were sharers in many of the exploits carried through by them—those at least of you who are of mature years—and the younger of you have heard of these deeds from your fathers. They are not such very ancient events nor of such a sort as to be forgotten through the lapse of time. Still, the eyewitness of those who have seen, testifies better than does the hearing of deeds that happened but yesterday or the day before."[1]

Meanwhile in Chania around the same time/chronos as the first men of Anatolia appeared at Edirne, a similar speech was

[1] Attributed to Byzantine historian Michael Kritovoulos.

given by Captain Michalis. He was the equivalent of a brigand. A man with a long flowing moustache joining a beard, dark skin, a scowling voice and piercing black eyes who could scare any child to bed if they misbehaved for their parents.

Michalis was a fierce Cretan, an island that technically belonged to the Venetian empire. Yet no one from Venice ever questioned his authority, collected his taxes or caused him any grief. He was always given a wide passage when Venetian authorities encountered him on a cobblestone street or a back alley of Chania.

After hearing from a messenger sent by Persephone in Monemvasia that the despots were not daring to leave the Morea and that an imminent attack on Constantinople was brewing, he gathered his fellow Cretans to brew a patriotic spirit.

With a few short words, 700 men and a small group of women pledged to fight to the death. Crete, just like Sparta, had women ready to fight. King Pyrrhus was of course, famously held by Spartan women when he invaded Laconia; the Spartan men were (coincidently) off in Crete for campaign season and it did not matter for the women were skilled and strong and fought off their assailants.

According to Persephone, speed was of the of the essence and by daybreak a boat supplied from the Venetians sailed out to Mytilene harbour. From Lesvos, the men and women would then cross over and make their way up the Asia Minor coast to join the defence of the city. This was a mission that would define them for they had always beaten pirates, Venetian police and others, and had never fought against the might of the Ottoman empire, led by a determined, youthful sultan.

Chapter 5

Flashback to the younger sultan

My name is Mehmed, and I want to be a conqueror. I am a European, for I was born in Edirne, yet my empire is essentially Asian. If I can add more European territory, I will feel as though it is multi continental. I want to change history, for my people, for Allah. For too long the infidel have held Constantinople. If I want to change history, honour my ancestors and eliminate my detractors, then I need to take Constantinople. I intend that nothing shall halt me.

An old prophecy foretold that the city would fall, therefore, why should it not fall to me?

My father had hoped to take the city. His name was Murad, yet he was too friendly to these Greeks. He took their gold, believed their lies and overestimated the threat of the Hungarians and the Pope, despite defeating them at Varna. He should have known that as long as the Latins practised Filioque[1] the Latins under the pope had incorporated into their church as a description for Holy Spirit procession and was part of the liturgy by 1014. Doctrinal

[1] Which means "and from the Son."

Figure 5.1: Portrait of the sultan. Image courtesy of Yolgezertan.

differences between Constantinople and Rome are best for others to provide a treatment on; their complexities and politics is beyond this paragraph to go into.

and had other doctrinal differences, the Christian states were not going to come cantering to the rescue of Constantinople. Think about it, how many wars had the Greeks fought against Latins, Franks, Venice, Catalans, Crusaders, Normans? No need to answer, for I know that the West is not really going to send military and aid to fight us. It would take a significant shift in mindset for those greedy westerners to come for me. Therefore the west is not the best for Constantinople.

My father should have crushed them all. My father was too soft.

However, he did allow me to govern the province of Amasya when I was 11, which was a decade ago and he made me study, thus gaining a strong understanding of my Islamic faith. I was trained in languages including Greek, and subjects that included science, mathematics and my teachers fostered a belief that the empire could only succeed if I overthrew Constantinople.

A year after becoming governor, my father abdicated, and I was Mehmed II, the ruler or the empire. Murad wanted a quiet life. Maybe hard decisions were not for him anymore. A few months later, the Hungarians under their tough leader, John Hunyadi led a crusade to Varna with the blessing of the white man in the Vatican.

Why my father thought it was a good idea that a boy, under the guidance of viziers with their own agendas, could defeat a determined enemy, I will never know.

The grand vizier helped me write a letter to my father in Asia, pleading with him to return to lead us against the Hungarians, who were guilty of breaking the peace treaty we had in place with them. How dare they break an agreement? This is not the way diplomacy should be. Note, we needed the treaty, in order to build up our Balkan possessions before we could consider breaking the treaty. Sadly, they simply beat us to it.

The grand vizier was a man named Çandarlı Halil Paşa. He was never well disposed to me. Maybe one day, "I will dispose of him," I had thought at the time. Anyway, my father received the letter and pleas at Manis and returned to rule and teach the Hungarians a valuable lesson at Varna on the Black Sea coast. Varna was a Greek city from the years of Greek colonists. Now it became a wasteland for their 'saviours.'

⋆⋆

When Murad died two years ago, I did what any good son would do.... I killed all my rival siblings. There was no way I was going to have a potential rival waiting out there, waiting to overthrow me in case I failed.

As soon as I was secure, my sole focus was not on finding a life partner or pursuing frivolous endeavours such as hunting or conquering more territory in Asia. I wanted the big prize.

I appointed Baltoghlu as admiral and drew a plan to double our fleet and prepare them to take the city. It meant many of our rowers and ship builders were recruited from Christian ranks, as we are not the best seafarers.

In the narrow straits leading the Black Sea, my grandfather had built the fortress Anadolu Hisari on the Asian side. It gave me an idea. I decided to build a castle on the other side replete with cannons and some of my best troops. I named it Rumeli Hisarı in honour of the territory I was seizing. I now had control of the straits. Yes I know, there was a treaty that said this was the land of the emperor. Well guess what, diplomacy was now being broken.

In the castle I stationed 400 Janissaries, which had four towers and a baker's dozen of watchtowers on the walls linking the main towers.

To generate some income and show that I meant business, I charged any ship passing through a toll. Most paid. Some of the clever Genoans and Venetians waited for strong winds and took their chance against my cannons.

Guess what? One day, a Venetian ship was gunned down for failing to stop. Those who weren't killed swam to shore. It didn't matter which side, we rounded them up, smiled and beheaded them. My local captain had the good sense to impale the Venetian captain, a certain Antonio Rizzo, to serve as a warning to others not to tempt fate. And for those in the Venice senate, try and take back the straits. My diplomacy will work. This is the way diplomacy should be.

Chapter 6

January arrival of Giustiniani

Who is he to the Greeks? Possibly their saviour, but for the purposes of our interaction dear reader, please use the name Giustiniani, a Genoan.

Genoa had become a distant mistress to the nobleman. A beautiful but distant lover, and over time, had become detached from her.

Chios had become more of a home for Giustiniani. The Greeks and Genoans decidedly made the co-existence work. The Genoese governed and provided a fleet against Venice or other predators and the Greeks went on their merry ways. As long as they paid taxes and kept producing a delicious, curious white delight that he could dip into a cup of water, then all was well between them.

One night, as the Genoan sat by the harbour in the company of some of his men and a bevy of beautiful Chiotean women, a runner sprinted up from a small galley that had anchored.

He headed straight for Governor Berlo. An animated conversation took place, with many hand gestures and the nodding of heads. Some may have wondered if any body parts were tired after the animated discussion.

The runner soon departed back to the galley.

Governor Berlo, was a stout and chubby man. Giustiniani once told me, “Berlo was not known for sudden movements. It is probable he hadn’t undertaken exercise since the time some of my men and I played a joke as he was sleeping at his casa. We burst into his casa and proclaimed that pirates had invaded! The look on his face as he yelled profanities and rushed out to see if it was true, was enough to make us all crumple on the ground in laughter.”

The Governor approached the Genoan at the table. This time there was no hint of a prank.

“Giovanni. . . .”

“Yes my trusty Governor?”

“The infidel is on the move.”

“Not to our fair island?”

“Alas, they have assembled a massive army, bigger than anything anyone has seen before. They are preparing for an attack on Constantinople from the Adrianople side.”

Processing what he had just heard. Giustiniani leant over to take a quick sip of the white element in his glass. “This is not good news. Christendom cannot withstand the loss of Constantinople, and with it, Galata will not be too far behind.”

“Captain, these are difficult times. We have the Knights of St John in Rhodes, not sure if we can count on them as allies. Venetians everywhere and the growing power of the young Sultan. We still need the Hellenes as a balance, as friends.”

“Christendom needs them too.” Sighing and looking at his men. In the background. A young but tough lot sprinkled with a number of veterans who had fought with him on a number of campaigns. Good men with families, and a strong sense of loyalty.

“Governor. I will provision a force of men. . . .”

The Governor cut the conversation off.... "We need you here to safeguard our island. The Greeks care not for the republics. In any case, they cannot beat the Sultan if the numbers I am hearing about are not misleading."

"Governor, you have the fleet and good defences. I am only going with the intention to have a coffee with the emperor and buy some wool from Galata. It is getting cold on Chios and I think the sheep here no longer want to give me the wool I need. I long ago gave up the brutal sport of hunting animals for clothes. This is a good chance to buy silk and other material."

With a wry smile, the governor embraced the Genoan. He may not necessarily want him to depart, he did however understand that as a Genoan, he would be welcomed by an ailing empire. The governor realised that this could be the last time they meet in a social setting.

The next day, Giustiniani sent out a call for any of the Greeks wanting to march or row to their probable deaths.

"I pride myself on picking men designed to cope mentally as well as emotionally. That day I put all the men to the test. Physical, combat, and character. You see, in a long siege, it is character that will dig you out of a hardship. The men could sing, play tavli, some could play musical instruments, and many could recite stories." Giustiniani wrote in his secret diary.

By the end of the day, 300 local men, including some from Rhodes, a number that would make Sparta and Thebes proud, had enlisted. Along with the 400 Genoans he already had at his disposal. He called them his familia, the Genoan would tell his friend the Latin Archbishop Leonard of Chios at a later time, who also kept a record of the siege for posterity. Leonard was in Mytilene at the time that Isodore sailed through and convinced him to join the expedition to Constantinople.

Leonard would recount that Giustiniani would explain, "my family is a rich one, all these men would be rewarded with payment direct to their families. We do not plunder the defeated, we use what we have rightfully earned in a civilised manner."

⋆ ⋆

On 1 February, Giustiniani and his troops set sail from Chios, making a stop in Mytilene to purchase grain and additional weapons for the fight ahead. Every member of the crew had a job. If they were not directly involved in the sailing tasks, they could sing, entertain or fish. One of the crew managed to snare a mermaid but let her go as he wasn't her type. Or was it the other way around?

Next, after sailing past Lemnos, opposing Telendos and Imvros, all possessions of the emperor, Giustiniani sailed past the straits of Gallipoli. Gallipoli is a name many will never forget.

Later that day, Giustiniani was asked by the crew why he stared intently at the coastline of Gallipoli. Here is what he told them:

"Gallipoli was settled in the 600s BC by Ionian and Aeolian settlers. Twelve cities were established on the peninsula of the Hellespont, an area also known as Thracian Chersonesus.

Over a century ago, Gallipoli was not yet formally in possession of the Ottoman Turks. It remained an Eastern Roman area, which was a two-day's march from Constantinople. Whilst Gallipoli may mean good or beautiful, there was nothing beautiful about the power and greed of many Hellenes last century. The empire was in decline thanks to disastrous losses to Ottoman Turks and the disgraceful Christian Fourth Crusade—and with friends like these who needs enemies!"

The empire was in the midst of a civil war, which gave the Ottomans a chance to intervene directly in Europe. Emperor John IV Kantakouzenos, who was either mad or simply out of options with his limited resources, sought the help of Orhan and his troops to deal with his adversaries, as well as taking on Serbian troops. Orhan was the son of the founder of the Ottoman Empire, Osman;

he also married a princess, Theodora. The civil war of 1352–1357 between John IV and John V resulted in enormous pillaging of Macedonia and to a lesser extent Thrace. The two warring leaders allowed this to happen under their watch as a way of paying off their new friends by looting some of the countryside!

As a result, Orhan was exposed to Europe. With John IV emerging victorious by 1352, the Turks were given temporary forts near Gallipoli to continue their pillaging. This was meant to be temporary and to repay the Ottomans. In my mind, I can only find one word to describe such a chaotic deal; madness. An absence of strategic thinking. Orhan simply built up his power and wealth. He harassed the Hellenes of the region and when an earthquake struck in 1354 destroying most of Gallipoli, he annexed the region. This was the first time a European territory was formally included in the Ottoman Empire, a blow from which the Empire and the Balkans did not recover from. John IV feebly protested. Inexplicably, the emperor somehow believed the sultan would play nice and return Gallipoli with some Turkish delights. He paid the price with his exile at the end of the year by John V.

From this moment on, Ottomans had a staging post to expand into Europe. Within eight years they had taken the large city of Adrianople (Edirne). From there, the Ottomans in Europe are hard to defeat.

The empire in the 1300s, though somewhat weakened, was still a force to be reckoned with. It remained viable and could have held out the Ottomans had they not conspired to destroy each other. The civil war was one of many during the last century. Ironically, Gallipoli was freed in 1366 with a mixture of forces loyal to the pope, troops from Lesvos under Gallitusio and troops led by the patriarch of Constantinople. A decade later after yet another civil war, the *Byzantine Empire* again lost Gallipoli. This time, it was simply given over by Andronikus, the son of John V, to the Ottomans as a payment for services rendered. Andronikus' name means victory of a man. Perhaps stupidity of a man would have been more suitable."

Giustiniani may have bored a few to sleep, and considering their insomnia, they were grateful. The rest were happy to hear his version of history, which had first been learned from a *friend* in the city years ago.

"And this is part of the context of why the Ottomans were marching on the most important city in Europe," Giustiniani now thought to himself as he watched the small waves crash into his ship. On either side he could see the lush green of two continents, hills, nature and eagles. *The eagles were coming.*

Chapter 7

The deeds of Giustiniani flashback

My name is Giovanni Giustiniani Longo, my Greek friends call me Ιωάννης and my Latin mates call me GG for short, though short I am not. I was born into the Genoese nobility around 1411 and I was a tall, tough kid. Start a fight with me and you will end up with broken bones and bruises aplenty. I found my way around various Genoese provinces, fighting an occasional battle and mastering my craft. The Black Sea and Sardinia taught me brutal lessons; how to fight on limited resources, sparingly employing your manpower until absolutely necessary as well as siege warfare. The Crimea, especially during a brutal winter could really test oneself. If the weather didn't get to you, some of the toothless women could. Or bears. I was always grateful to undertake my duties and then quickly take off out of the Crimea, though it is fair to say that Avars, Rus, Saracens, Scythians and a range of others were never any match for my tactics.

I must have won dozens of battles. I had kept score until I matched Alexander the Great's tally. Growing up in Genoa, as a republic with ties to the Pope, we had little affinity with the Greeks of the East Roman Empire. They were an autocracy; they had their own patriarch and had a taste for pork. Peculiar.

I first visited Constantinople on a journey home from the Black Sea in 1441 or thereabouts, on a beautiful, cloudless day just after the feast day for the Holy Virgin. Since 1320 my countrymen had established a walled colony opposite Constantinople called Galata. This is the Greek word for milk, though, cows and dairy weren't exactly our trading strength. The small colony was granted by the emperor as their power had waned. With the growth of Venetian power and the threat of the Ottomans on the horizon, along with incessant civil wars, it made sense that we had been allowed to establish Galata. This came via a commercial agreement with Constantinople and despite not being allowed to fortify, we did build walls! Note, we are no friends of Venice, though a few do live in Galata, along with a small group of Jews and some Greeks. The colony sits on the shores of the Golden Horn, opposite Constantinople, in anticipation of the eventual foray of the Turks. Some would say we are the insurance policy, a safety net for the Greeks. When my small flotilla of vessels entered the Sea of Marmara we were immediately impressed by the high towers and large outer walls that greet you on one side, and the smaller walled colony of Galata. Both had used stone and masonry of the highest order.

I decided to anchor our boats in the harbour of the great city. After my first ship mate dealt with formalities with the master of the harbour, one by one 80% of each boat was allowed to disembark. A standard practise is to never leave your berth unattended. Greeks, Venetians, Neapolitans, Catalans, Arabs. You can't trust anyone.

The men had free range and shore leave for two days. Some of them took the time to practise their love making techniques. "It was for their anxious wives left behind in Genoa or the Black Sea, best to be in practise," they explained. Good men, who seemed to want to be battle hardened for that reunion of 'love and lust.'

As a young captain, with no attachments and baggage, I knew that my luck would come with a visit to one of countless drink houses, should I wish that to be the case. The chance to explore one of the most intriguing cities in history, survey the land foundations, visit the churches and monuments was just too good an opportunity to knock back; and that is what I did. I went searching for one called the Hippodrome, a Greek word for horses.

I stood by the hippodrome, it was breathtaking, despite the fact it wasn't that well-tended. This is where the blues and greens had fought for sporting and supremacy, including the brutal Nika riots in 453AD that resulted in tens of thousands of deaths. Who needs a virus or a plague, when you can just kill each other? The venue was like the Coliseum, which could fit almost 50,000 spectators in its prime. Sadly, the equivalent of the current population of Constantinople.

Still amazed to be standing next to the famed Hippodrome, I didn't notice the person next to me who was invisible to this point.

"Italiano?" came a faint voice.

"Si, Genoa. Though I haven't seen my home city since I was made a sea captain at the age of 20."

"Why did you not disembark and stay at Galata? Men from the republics are not always welcome here," she asked from under her long dark eye lashes.

"I see."

"Captain, your kind brought about ruin to a great city. The 1204 and 1205 betrayal by Venice has meant our city has declined every decade since, as you can see from the unkept Hippodrome."

"When was the last time the venue was used?" My brows were now furrowing.

"Genoan, the Greeks stopped using this venue for sports endeavours some years after Michael Palaiologos took the city back, with the help of our great protector, the Holy Virgin in the year of 1261." Continuing, the strange woman added, "many thespians have since used the venue as a place to rehearse and perform theatre."

"Your people look down upon prostitution and theatre, seeing them as similar lowly professions," I stated.

"Yes senor. I am in theatre. It was in the blood of my ancestors and it enables me to gain a sense of freedom that few like me will ever gain." She straightened her back imperceptibly.

"What do you mean?"

"This great Constantinople has seen many an empress rule. In society though, we remain with a limited voice. I feel the equal to any man when I perform. Rather than be lowly, it makes us equal. More!" She explained to me.

"You are a Greek?" I asked with surprise.

"My father is a Greek; my mother is a servant brought here by barbaric traders from Africa. She is from Ethiopia."

I was intrigued by the woman in front of me. Long black hair, pretty brown eyes, curvaceous with luscious red lips. Suddenly I sensed what many of my men had wanted. I pushed any thoughts away and continued the conversation with the stranger.

As the young woman spoke to me, she explained her father is a fighter and had served under the Despot of the Morea, Constantine, prince of Constantinople. His name is Theodoros.

This prompted me to ask about the land walls which had been built to the current stature by the emperor Theodosian a thousand years earlier; the early days of the empire.

"I need to visit the land walls. Can you escort me?" I asked, perhaps with an ulterior motive.

"Paisano, some people may talk." Pausing, and looking around with a degree of fake acting. "Fortunately for you, they already talk about us thespian performers, therefore I can take you around the city. My father taught me a lot about the walls, ramparts, the ditches. . . . and the evil men from the republics! You know that it was the Greeks who came up with the term Italy 1400 years ago?"

"And it was those same Italians or Romans who started calling you Greek, in honour of some obscure tribe in Epiros, the Graeci, I believe!" He smiled as his ability to remember some of the history lessons he learned as a boy in Genoa.

As the day light met the evening shadows, two strangers surveyed the land walls. I was impressed by the knowledge and understanding of his newfound friend. As an actress, she had absorbed the information her father had told her and recounted the facts to her friends and relatives.

As an early evening moon crept into the background, standing on top of one of the great towers facing the Blachernae Palace, I leant down. I couldn't resist feeling powerful over such a petite woman, a metaphor for the giant walls of what had now seemed like a shrunken city; a city that now consisted of just two lonely, entwined souls.

⋆ ⋆

Along the walk, every time our eyes met, she flinched, and when I leant towards her, suddenly she was out of breath. Next second, her balance was also gone. On a reflex, I held her, one hand on her arm, the other on her waist. Trying to keep her from falling, I brought her soft body against mine, forcing our eyes to meet once again, closely. A kiss was exchanged before we could avoid it, a resistance, I think, neither of us would want to put up.

Neither of us were aware of what this solitaire play would reserve for its ending. For their own amusement, the gods of theatre fed its faithful servant with words she shared without analysing possible risks:

"You've been through a long journey, captain. You deserve a warm bath. . . "

We walked side by side to her humble house. She poured a drink from Lesvos so I could sip and delight myself while she prepared it's unexpected guest a bath. Once it was ready, the small, beautiful intelligent woman helped me to become just a man. Shedding the clothes, protections and dropping my weapons. Another kiss, deeper and with a dash of desperation. This time I could feel better her soft body, hair and scent. I felt a rush towards taking her clothes off, but, once again, I pushed my instincts, as I could really use a bath first.

She turned around as I stepped into the hot water. My fluttering shadow, projected by the fire, passed over her and the wall she was facing. She sat on a chair close by, gently rubbed my back, my shoulders, my chest. Once she felt the muscles were loose, the actress decided to leave me alone so I could close my eyes for a few minutes.

As the water got a bit colder, I stepped out of the tub finding a clean towel and comfortable clothes over the chair (I wondered whose clothes I was going to use. Hopefully, not a husband...). I took the towel but never really touched the clothes. Despite the cool breeze outside, I felt warm and the rush for taking her clothes off came back. Stronger.

I opened the bathroom door finding a goddess with brown skin, long black hair down, fresh clothes showing off her perfect curvy silhouette. We met halfway, both breathing heavily.

The marathon was just beginning.

⋆⋆

I met her one more time, at the taverna for another all-night discussion before his own shore leave was up.

Bidding farewell to "my very own Greek Goddess," I made my way hurriedly back to the harbour, before the gates of the city could shut.

As I walked around the bend of the first gate, I bumped into a gruff and grim looking man, pale and almost lost in his thoughts.

"I'm sorry." I said as I towered over a man carrying what appeared to be a diary. I held out my hand to lift the fallen man.

"Thank you kind sir. Genoan?"

"Si Senor."

"Are they your sloops in our harbour Genoan?

I nodded.

"Very impressive. I am George Sphrantzes, secretary to the emperor."

"I am Giustiniani Longo, of the House of Doria, Genoa."

"Welcome to the city."

We exchanged further pleasantries. Sphrantzes only allowing me to leave on the condition of returning to visit the city and the emperor whenever the winds bring me back.

"Where are you heading to next captain?" Sphrantzes asked.

"I will need to visit our Genoese island of Chios where I stay when I am not on duty."

"Do you like these islands of the Greeks?"

"Senor Sphrantzes, they remind me of Genoa, a place I have not seen for many years. I have a love and a bond with Chios. The people are family, we are one."

"Have you been to other islands, nisia?" Sphrantzes enquired.

"Almost ten years ago we joined a military expedition led by the Greeks of Constantinople to take a pirate stronghold. The pirate force had taken a small citadel on Molyvos, which is on the island of Lesvos, which you would know. An excellent fortress with a very large band of well-trained pirates and renegades. Our numbers were much smaller. I had the pleasure of leading 200 Genoese troops to storm the citadel. We took it in less than a week."

"Captain, I had heard of this success. The fortress I believe is ancient and at the top of a small mountain, sitting above a beautiful town and harbour. These pirates had raided Chios the previous year. Well next time you return, I would like to hear more about your successes and bravery."

"Grazie. I hope we meet again soon, and may it always be under pleasant circumstances!"

Chapter 8

Emperor and Theodora

The bad luck and tragedy experienced by the emperor with his first and second wives, would be enough to destroy any man. Unlike many contemporary males, Constantine was always willing to listen to women and talk to them. His mother taught him to respect all people, including women. The empire had seen many great women rulers in an official capacity, such as Empress Irene, and unofficial as a regent or wife of an emperor. Justinian truly became great with the help, counsel and support he received from his wife, Theodora.

Therefore it was ironic that in his time of comfort, aside from Sphrantzes and Notaras, he could rely on another Theodora in a similar way that Justinian was able to. The other woman who had been significant in his life was his mother. Helena was caring, strong, a good counsel and able to display huge reserves of courage and strength. There is no doubt whom the emperor had predominantly taken after.

When the ills and travails of the empire wasn't consuming his thoughts, he would be thinking of his Theodora. A curvaceous, tall woman, who almost met the charismatic Constantine in height.

Her darker features complimented his. A kiss from Theodora was all he needed to turn his day's fortunes around. Having met at a party given in his honour, by her much older cousin Notaras, the two immediately were drawn to each other. The emperor was not shy of talking to a beautiful woman or dancing with her.

Theodora had been schooled in geography, philosophy and history, and had travelled with her older cousin, Lukas Notaras, to territories occupied by the Ottomans. Thus the emperor had a number of reasons to call upon Theodora to be in her company. Geography? Information about the towns, roads and infrastructure of the Ottomans. Soon enough, he was able to gain enough of a time passport with Theodora, and so certain that he asked her to marry him. For he was not only drawn to her vast knowledge, he was attracted to her from almost the first moment he met her.

⋆ ⋆

After another day at the imperial palace discussing strategies and politics with his counsel, including Notaras and Sphrantzes, he bade his friend good night and then said good evening to a lesson in world history as Theodora joined him for that one evening that they could escape the empire and simply be together. Their eyes twinkled as the met in the moonlight.

Dinner faded into wine and wine faded into a rare evening of passion.

The emperor's chamber had a magnificent sea view, complimented in a new moon's night. Constantine closed the door, took a slow breath, pushing away worries that insistently came across his mind. Turned around finding Theodora sipping wine by the window, mesmerized by the stars she knew so well. A dozen candles were lit across the room, but it was hardly enlightened. Still, somehow, Theodora's figure seemed to draw the perfect light to her.

"Which path are the stars are pointing, my love?"

"They don't point to anything, agapi mou. We need to choose our destiny, and once we do, the right stars will find us."

Approaching Theodora, touching her face, her hair. He knew her destiny would be in the direction of Trebizond, he uttered into her ear, "which star should I thank for your path crossing mine?

They kissed, gently, at first, then urgently. Constantine was intoxicated, not by the wine, but her perfume, olive skin, hair and curves. They made love under the light of a dozen candles and a thousand stars. There was a need to rush under the circumstances; and a drop of desperation only true love and lust combined can forge.

The fresh breeze coming across the window brought the ocean smell as a sweet remembrance that things you don't see, can still exist.

Chapter 9

Flight to Trebizond

"Theodora I need this favour from you. It is a dangerous voyage." The emperor said urgently.

"Constantine, this is not how I want to spend the next few weeks, as those crazies try to take my city. . . ." His voice trailing away.

"King David II Komnenos is very much an East Roman; a Greek and a friend of our empire. Trebizond and her people are essentially part of our extended family. They will come for his empire next. We need his support. His connection with the Georgians could also help us, we need them both. In fact, a long time ago their Queen Tamar provided invaluable support to the fledgling Trebizond empire. In fact, there have been Greeks as monarchs in their lands. Look, we need ships and any food supplies they can muster to sail down the Bosporus."

"I understand my love, but I want to be here with you, with us, our people." She confessed.

The emperor didn't want to lose one more love in his life. She was too precious to him. He would miss her smile, the touch, her scent. Also, he could not spare too many others. She was strong willed, bossy at times and would steer the small crew perfectly to David.

"Is that the sealed letter that George provided earlier?" She asked with a sigh.

He nodded. "Theodora, speed is of the essence. If Venice sends ships and supplies and possibly the Hungarians, we will survive. And if we do, our local bard will make a song called, *I will survive* for us to remember and cherish the victory. If they do not, we need Trebizond and any other entity to come to our aid." In the same breath he added, "remember, you need to stay at Trebizond, you mustn't attempt to return unless it is safe. This is not open for discussion. If we fail, you will be needed to advise the King on how they can best defeat the enemy. Understood?"

With tears running down her cheeks, she moved closer to the emperor. She did not answer his question as she landed a passionate kiss as everything else went blank around them.

⋆⋆

As a small crew was hastily assembled inside the boom of the harbour, one of the younger members asked an elderly man, the 'captain,' what Trebizond was? This was to be his maiden trip to the Black Sea.

In a scraggy voice that had seen many a sea in his long life, the newly appointed captain started, "Son, Trebizond is a city that was founded in the eighth century BC by Greek colonists from Miletus on the Black Sea coast in northern Asia Minor which became known as the Pontus region. Xenophon in his classic fourth century BC book, 'Anabasis' describes the joy of his troops as they finally encountered a Greek city after a long and treacherous march from Persia encountering enemy and foreign countries. Trebizond prospered under the rule of Mithridates and the Pontian kings during the first century AD and was an important port for trade during the East Roman years which commenced around 330AD.

In 1204, after many years of civil war and feuding, Constantinople was taken by the Crusaders through deception, aided and abetted by Emperor Isaac II Angelos for personal gain. A number of Greek successor states emerged; the Greeks of Nicaea in Asia Minor, who would win back Constantinople in 1261 (restoring the empire), the Greeks of Epiros who would be absorbed by the Nicaeans and the Empire of Trebizond.

If we backtrack to 1185, the Byzantine Emperor Andronikus I was overthrown, and his family escaped to Georgia and the protection of Queen Tamar. In 1204 she provided Alexios I Komnenos (Andronikus' grandson and her nephew) with troops to capture the Pontian cities in and around Trebizond. Alexios proclaimed himself Megas Komnenos (Grand Komnenos) and the 'true' emperor of Byzantium. He was able to conquer a significant area on the Black Sea, from the borders of Georgia in the east to Sinope in the west. He also captured the Crimean Peninsula in what is now in the Ukraine."

"Sir, the Crimean is near Ukraine?"

"Eh, indeed. As for Alexios, he never effectively controlled more than 100km south of the capital. However this was to his advantage for beyond the high range mountains that Xenophon and his men once encountered, lay some of the most powerful enemies in the region. They included the Seljuk Turks, followed by the Mongols, a number of Turkish fiefdoms and ultimately the Ottomans. Thus Trebizond was fortunate to be protected by its natural position, the friendship of the Georgians, a series of alliances with Turkish princes, the Mongols, and the restored empire. Also, a reasonably strong economy.

During the reign of John II about 180 years earlier the empire reconciled itself with the city and ended its pretensions and claims to Constantinople and the entire Greek world. By 1282 the King of Trebizond was known by the title of 'Faithful Emperor and Autocrat of the whole of the East, the Iberians and the overseas province.'"

The younger member of the crew seemed fascinated by the history lesson, though some of the others helping assemble supplies feigned 'sleep!"

It was to this empire that Constantine hoped could respond before the Venetians arrived. If, they were to arrive. Theodora had an important task ahead as the fate of an empire hung in the balance.

Chapter 10

Grant the Scot

It was a typical Scottish day, just before the start of summer. Cold, windy, rainy, and then of course the sun came out. This phenomenon repeated over and over again. As I made my way, alone, in the Scottish Highlands, I couldn't help but think of how blessed I was. The rolling countryside and friendliness of my fellow Scots, our hatred for all things English and our love of a drink and a song. I had recently returned from another siege against the English, bringing down a castle with hall walls thanks to my ability to mine tunnels.

It was a skill I picked up as a young lad. Always getting into a wee bit of trouble from my parents, enough trouble that I used to dig mines to hide. It came naturally to me. It was also a good way to escape a rowdy gathering if you know what I mean.

My name is Johannes Grant, though to my friends in Constantinople, I am Grant the Scot. Occasionally, I am called a German, which always grates on my nerve. Look, I spent two years there creating mines for these tall, miserable sots. They always seem to owe people reparations, yet never fully pay them. I would rather be called English than say Bavarian or Frankish. When my work with them concluded, I somehow made my way, alone, just as I had in the Highlands, to the city of Constantinople to fight for Constantine. I had heard that the city was in danger and danger was one of my names, at least that is what they called me in Poland. Again, just don't call me Germania, or English and you and I can be friends.

You see, all that I need is good company, a drink, the sea as we never had that in the Highlands, and beautiful women. With my red hair, skeletal appearance and ginger beard, I seem to have fascinated the Greeks of the city upon my arrival.

The only other city that has intrigued me as much, is Edinburgh which is a stone paved and romantic place. One could propose to their partner here (as I once nearly did to a lass) or just get lost amongst the amazing array of beautiful buildings. In some respects, it is quite similar to what I would come across in some of the bigger Greek cities. And of course there is a certain warmth and charm about the Scottish people, traits you will similarly find amongst the Greek people.

I also wanted to see Greek theatre which I had heard about and I was privileged to watch a talented actress and her troupe. No, I did not make any moves, for her husband would not have been pleased.

Anyway, I have always marvelled at how resilient the Greek people are, they laugh in the face of adversity, and they understand the concept of being strong willed and proud. Traits that also held in high regard throughout the Scottish world. In some respects, the distinct culture of Scotland is somewhat similar to Greece. Just think about 'philoxinea' (Greek hospitality), the Kilt which is a mini version of the toga (the traditional Greek and Roman dress for men), the ability to have a good time even when times are tough, and the resilience of both people. Admittedly, we are less hairy than either men or women of Greek extraction.

When I turned 40, I booked my express donkey and travelled

through the Holy Roman Empire, then

via the Hungarians and down the Black Sea to the Sea of Marmara. Being brash, I tried to knock out a Varangian Guard who wouldn't let me into the city, though I am not sure if that was what he was saying, oh yeah, he may have actually said *welcome to Constantinople how may I.....*

After bruising my hand, I was surrounded by serious looking buffed up lads.... who suddenly laughed and laughed at this skinny ginger haired man attempting to pick a fight with a seven-foot giant. Despite my bruised ego and the commotion, a well-dressed man with silver hair approached me and spoke in Latin.

Sphrantzes introduced himself, asking who I was.

After explaining that I was an adventurer from Scotland and Germany, an intrigued secretary motioned me to follow him. Polite conversation followed us until we reached what can only be described as an Edinburgh building built by the heavens, the Blachernae Palace.

And then I met the man who would change my life. All dressed in purple.

Chapter 11

Emperor and the defences

It is not all that it is cracked up to be, an emperor. You have to wear purple. Not exactly a favourite colour, though it is the colour though of my favourite singer/bard. You have to be a diplomat, a warrior, a treasurer, God's representative on earth and hope you don't offend any nobles or generals enough to lead to civil war. You probably know that Greeks enjoy a good civil war.

Greeks fighting Greeks, this has always been a constant. Sparta vs Athens or anyone, Syracuse vs other Greek cities in Magna Graecia, the post Alexander Hellenic Age kingdoms, and now during the last two centuries, Constantinople had experienced wars amongst our countryfolk. This had weakened us. More importantly, my empire was fragmented. We had territory in central Greece, the Morea, islands, Thrace. These are disparate parts. Hard to defend and all over the place. A century ago we still held territory in certain areas of Asia Minor and the Black Sea, Macedonia and Epiros. They are long gone to the sultan, Serbians, Bulgarians and Italian Republics.

When Constantine was being confirmed as the emperor, one of his brothers tried to steal the title and hurried to Constantinople before us. Fortunately, his dear mother Helena, a Serbian by birth, always trusted Constantine. She stalled his brother Demetrius from any attempt to be crowned emperor. It did not end there, as the emperor of a shrunken and weakened empire, I had to make his way to see sultan Murad II for an *aye or nay* to accept the appointment. This is the world I live in; it's not cracked up to what it should be for a 'grand, autocrat' emperor.

The emperor has this once great city to defend against what can only be described as a million devils. Some would say they are as numerous as the stars.[1]

And here we are, on the verge of a siege. After meeting Giustiniani, we decided to divide the city into fourteen areas for defence and a plan for a fightback. The emperor planned this with a non-resident Genoan, that is how far the empire has fallen. Anyway, more on that later.

[1]*As numerous as the stars* is a reference to a chapter of the same name by Roger Crowley about Byzantium and stars they are not.

Chapter 12

Another Flashback: Grant and his companion

Writing in his diary, the Scot noted his encounter with the emperor, "nothing compares to meeting a monarch. Strong, imposing, charismatic and worldly. His father had made it to London a few decades earlier on a mission to raise awareness and support against Murad, the then sultan. Alas, to no avail. Just as well as I would not have helped any man who was actively engaged with the English. They can all rot, and I don't just mean their teeth."

"Johannes, I had heard of an engineer who made his way to our lands via the coast of the Black Sea." The emperor stared at me, "where you caught your ship, where the Danube meets the sea, this was once one of our many boundaries." The emperor, paused in thought.

"If only we still held the lands. Son, our empire may be weak, but we have spies everywhere. We maintain a program of Dimitris 001 all the way through to Dimitris 009. They are our secret agents. We learn information and then we try to use gold or diplomacy to solve an issue or an impending threat."

Having looked around the once great city, Grant was perplexed about the mention of gold.

"Therefore I knew you were coming. In Germania, we once had a princess of ours become a Queen there, Sophia. She introduced the concept of a fork to them. In turn, they called us Hellenes, thinking it was derogatory. We try to teach them civilisation and they think they will try to insult us. Well, we are Romans by virtue of empire and Constantine the Great; no relation to Alexander. And we are Hellenes by choice, blood."[1]

"Sir, your highness. . . ."

"Here you are amongst friends. Please call me God!"

Sphrantzes and the emperor burst out laughing.

"He prefers Constantine amongst friends. In public, we address Constantine as emperor, baslieus," explained Sphrantzes.

Grant smiled. Then smiled even more broadly. "Now that we have that out of the way, what can I drink my new friends?" The Scot, wasting no time to indulge in local drinking etiquette among "friends!"

Before the emperor could turn his head to a court assistant, out walked what can only be described as an Aphrodite. Grant was stunned, knees seemingly a little weak as he tried to keep himself upright. Feigning little interest in the woman, he asked his question again, before Sphrantzes explained this was an Armenian servant of the Blachernae Palace.

"Irene has been a loyal employee of the palace, the emperor and God for many years. Her grandparents were refugees from 63 years earlier when the Ottomans took Philadelphia. This was the last remaining city of our empire in Asia Minor, notwithstanding Trebizond."

---

[1]'Hellenes' was considered a derogatory term by the Franks. In the first few centuries of the Byzantine Empire, to be a Hellene meant pagan. By and large the citizens were Roman until a slow cultural awakening by many Greeks in the last few centuries.

Constantine offered, "the people of Philadelphia, which means a city of friends, were brave. They held out, surrounded entirely for years by the enemy. Her grandparents were amongst a small group of survivors and they brought back with them information about how they held out, what survival techniques the Philadelphians used and sacred icons."

Turning, the Armenian woman said, "I am treated like one of the family. All of my family since they first arrived here." A voice of an angel chimed in, the Scot thought. She was comfortable that the emperor would not frown on her timely addition to the conversation.

"In fact, there are many Armenian people across the empire and in Asia Minor. Like the Assyrians, Georgians, Pontians and other Christians, we remain the majority in Asia Minor. Sadly, we do not have the military strength, and many have started to convert to the religion of the Turkmen. Some because they are afraid, and others to avoid paying taxes. Only Christians pay tax." She continued with vigour.

"And then of course there is a tax on families, where the sultan takes Christian boys and raises them in the Janissary corps. This is the most barbaric element. These boys then grow up pledging allegiance only to the sultan and are trained as fierce warriors. Many are sent to fight in the lands whence they were taken from. It's tragic," offered Sphrantzes with his recently acquired perpetual frown.

Grant whose head was spinning from the information, asked loudly, "any other stories or propaganda you have for this Scottish Pagan, otherwise can you pour this thirsty wee lad something?!"

The room burst out in laughter.

Grant, having spent many of his recent years in dark tunnels and darker places, suddenly felt as though a light was shone onto his empty heart. Or was it the alcohol.... Which had yet to be poured.

As the afternoon wore on, more stories were shared until the emperor was comfortable that he gained a special ally and friend for the campaign ahead. “Irene, could you see to it that our guest is given a room, one with a view to the water. Perhaps we can also find him some local dress as it will be cold here tomorrow, too cold for a kilt with chicken legs.

Considering his pale white legs lacked the hair of most Greek men, it would surely have created a chill for the Scotsman.

Chapter 13

Cretans have landed

The small flotilla from Mytilene harbour, to the Greek populated city of Aivali, took just a few short hours. It can always be a difficult crossing, and it is one that locals generally encourage foreigners not to undertake.

The Cretans were ready for war, mostly dressed with black trousers, black stivania boots, black sariki on their heads, shirts with a gold neck chain and thick black belt for their spathia blades.

Captain Michalis landed in a small town outside of Aivali in the early hours of the morning. He bade farewell to the crew who brought his men to the shores of Asia Minor, and urged them to visit the Knights of St John headquartered in Rhodes for help.

He would never be sure if the crew ever followed up on his request.

The disciplined group of Cretans dressed in black, were the last thing that the Ottoman garrison were expecting. Most able men had made their way to fight the sultan. None of the Greeks in the town were causing trouble. As long as they paid their taxes, they were left unmolested. Certainly, across the Asia Minor seaboard, Muslims and Christians were living peacefully, side by side. Certainly, the Ottomans needed the Christians for unlike Muslims, they were not exempt from paying tax and they were the ones running businesses and trading.

Michalis was well versed on the art of war. He knew the stealth and encircling techniques used by Alexander the Great when he led his Hellenes into Asia Minor. Michalis essentially encircled the entire barracks, and unlike Alexander, had minimal resistance as the few sentries on guard were easily taken out. The soldiers did their best to rouse from sleep. One by one, they were easily dealt with by the hungry and energetic Cretans.

Within twenty minutes, the garrison, which consisted of several hundred soldiers, was rounded up.... those who were not killed in the initial action.

Michalis did not need to provide any instructions. They instinctively knew to take all weapons and supplies. Michalis then addressed the prisoners.

"Sit down if you wish to live." No one could actually stand up as they were bound by their ankles and lying on the ground, not too dissimilar to a Persian carpet. "I see you all prefer to live. We can throw you in the Aegean Sea or we can let you return to your cities and towns; on the proviso you never take up arms against the empire or allies again."

Most of the troops could speak some level of Greek, the language understood by almost everyone in both empires.

The soldiers readily nodded.

If I ever hear that you are fighting again, I will come and find you. When a Cretan gives his or her word, we follow up or we have no honour. I will follow up if I have to.

Again a chorus of nods and "nai, nai."

As the Cretans departed on newly acquired horses, the captain untied his equivalent, bade him 'farewell' and provided him with a knife to unbound the prisoners.

The Cretans had a reputation of being the toughest of warriors.

The Ottoman captain was not prepared for this level of clemency, as he shed a tear knowing that he will once again see his nine children in Smyrna, where he will scurry to as soon as he frees the men.

Chapter 14

Arrival

The Cretans were the embodiment of stealth, as if winged angels on a mission from God. They cantered past ancient Troy and to the coastline opposite Gallipoli. Flat terrain greeted them as they continued to ride barely taking breath, stopping only to destroy a small garrison nine kilometres from Galata, to take their supplies, which included a tasty delicacy known as bak with lava.

As they decamped at the entrance to Galata, Captain Michalis approached the closed gate and asked to speak to the commander of the city.

"Commander, I am Captain Michalis, leader of the Cretans and a subject of Venice. I humbly ask, scrap that, I demand free passage across to Constantinople, food for my troops and any resources you can spare for the city."

"Captain, we are technically a neutral party to the impending siege..... neutral in every respect except for the fact some of our men have slipped into the city to help and we have affixed a chain from our walls to theirs to block the Golden Horn from Baltoghlu, the admiral. The chain is unable to be breached unless we detach it."

"Very well commander, that neutrality is duly noted!" He scowled, momentarily frightening those around him.

The Commander took a step back. "We had heard you were marching up the coast. The emperor's spies in the Dimitris program had informed us. We have prepared meals for you. As soon as you finish, our transports will take you across, with some care supplies for Sphrantzes. We will then resume our 'neutrality' as we know we are not a match for the Ottomans. When you cross over, Giustiniani, a Genoan, will be waiting for you and he will assign several towers to defend."

The Cretans were now ready for their destiny. Michalis had never lost a battle. He had no intention of defeat, none.

⋆⋆

The march, through the latter part of March from Edirne had been precision organisation and impressive despite the driving rain. Organised in every respect. The sultan and his viziers had everything covered. A team of land clearers and pavers had ridden ahead to ensure roads and passageways were smooth enough for the marchers and carts. Amongst the travellers, the sultan had included mobile hospitals, infectious disease experts as there was always a chance of disease amongst almost 200,000 people. This figure was made up of soldiers, administrators, support staff for the operation, hangers on, religious leaders, cooks, shepherds for the animals and engineers. Impressive in that such big numbers were disciplined enough not to deviate from the march, which remained orderly. If only some of the latter crusaders had been this disciplined in times gone by, particularly in the era of Alexios Komnenos. Every evening, the campfires gave an impressive demonstration of a carnival like atmosphere as people ate, prayed and practised drills.

Mehmed sent dozens of small unit across Thrace with the purpose of pillaging towns and looking out for any enemy troop movements. He was disappointed that a small band of Greeks, personally led apparently by the emperor and his consort had beaten two detachments of soldiers.

"Why couldn't that foolish emperor simply stay behind his men and behind the high walls," he thought. He himself was a thinker and a leader, not a foolhardy adventurer willing to lose his life in a silly sortie. Though he had grown up on Alexander the Great and other inspirational Greek and non-Greek leaders, there was no way he would be leading the frontline. No wonder Alexander, Brassidas, Achilles and many like him died young. "Only the good die young? No, only the careless do."

Sitting inside the grand tent, which was surrounded by Janissaries, the Sultan and Hilal Pasha held counsel. Hilal had not been in favour of the campaign; he was a wise old head who preferred a balance with the "stupid Greeks," as he often called them. "These stupid Greeks, they won't stop provoking, they never learnt to quit when they are behind!"

Hilal reminded the Sultan, as is the custom on a Holy campaign that he had explained to the enemy that if they surrender, no harm will come to the emperor or the citizens of Constantinople.

An emissary had visited the emperor, who had just returned to camp. Hilal brought him before Mehmed.

"Speak now and tell us what you have learned." Hilal motioned for the emissary to come forward as Mehmed and his advisors sat around a small buffet on the floor, sipping their tsai from silver cups.

"My sultan, the emperor brings you greetings. He has advised that it is you who should leave his lands. He will not surrender the city. I advised what the consequences will be if he chose to fight. They are preparing for a siege, though with what appears to be limited soldiers," concluding the verbal report.

"Dismissed," Hilal motioned to the man who promptly left the well-lit tent.

The sultan did not speak further of the matter that evening.

The next morning, a small embassy arrived at the camp, a mixed bag of men and women who were at an advanced age. An indicator that the emperor wasn't willing to spare his younger soldiers to speak to a bull headed, stubborn sultan intent on war.

The group dismounted and were escorted by Hilal. After a private conversation with Hilal lasting a few minutes, they were brought before the sultan.

"We bid you greetings from the emperor, who has graciously sent to you a number of gifts."

A number of gold plates were presented along with a writing pad and an ink pen. A copy of work by Homer was also presented.

The emissary continued, "the emperor requests you leave his lands and no harm will come to you or your troops. We request that Rumeli Hisar be dismantled and further request that you pay a greater upkeep for Prince Orhan or he will be released into Anatolia. Should you fail to comply, we will not stop until the Ottoman is no longer in Europe. For a thousand years we have protected Europe from the eastern hordes. We will continue to protect Europe."

Typical diplomacy from Byzantium, a mixture of bribery and threats. Although, this time the threats were empty. The sultan may as well have uttered the words, *stupid Greeks.*

He motioned to his Janissaries.

In an instant, all but one of the emperor's representatives were slain.

"You tell your emperor, he brought this upon himself," he scowled.

The trembling, remaining ambassador, made a hasty exit. Hilal, somewhat shocked, followed the older woman outside.

⋆ ⋆

Several days later on the sixth day of April, the Sultan ordered the dead ambassadors and other prisoners to be brought to the front of the walls. Those that were alive, prisoners captured from Thracian towns, were executed in front of the city.

This gruesome event made the defenders uneasy. For many it reinforced the barbaric nature of the sultan.

The emperor, shedding a tear for these innocent people was enraged.

In retaliation, he ordered 90 of his Ottoman prisoners to be hung from the ramparts facing the European side of Constantinople. Both leaders had shown a ruthless streak, a streak which had been hitherto absent from the emperor.

That evening, the first night of the Ottoman camp, was a joyous one. Music, prayer and food made their way around the camp. The Serbian allies were the least enthused about what had transpired. Unnecessary deaths to go along with no desire to be fighting for the sultan.

Inside the city, there was an element of despair. Most people attended a church service and prayed that Mehmed would be turned back whence he came.

There was to be more despair for the people, despite their attendance in church, for when they returned to the walls, they were confronted with the largest cannon the world had ever seen or experienced. It had taken many oxen and men to deliver the cannon from Edirne and it was to take many men every five hours to reload. For the sultan, it was worth the wait, for each ball smashed in the Theodosian walls caused enough damage to worry the defenders, especially Giustiniani. The defenders in turn called the cannon, the Basilica, as in the *royal cannon.*

There was a second cannon of similar size. His general, Zaganos Pasha, positioned a battery of cannons in the Lycus valley, deemed the easiest part of the city to attack due to the slope in the valley. The Saint Romanus Gate was the target, a chance to weaken the walls and gate by blasting as many cannons as they could at this one point.

Over a six-day period the bombardment was unrelenting. The leader observed all this, with no hint of a smile to betray his mood, he watched from his red and gold tent.

Each night, every citizen was tasked with the repairing of a section of the wall. Sphrantzes, Grant and Giustiniani divided the walls amongst the citizenry to repair the damaged walls. Young and old, women and men, priests or fighters, everyone was assigned a section and resources were available from Sphrantzes and the Italian merchants, who rather surprisingly were not asking for a fee!

The damage from the Basilica cannon every few hours was lasting. It stretched the resources of the emperor and frightened many of the defenders. It gave the invaders plenty of hope.

Over the course of these days before the shock, horror and awe, Zaganos sent troops to take any hold out towns including Therapia, a fort to the north of the city. Despite a strong resistance, the little fort on the sea was taken with a mixture of cannon and a larger force. Those who were not lost in the battle, were nonetheless lost to slavery. A good little money earner for the invaders.

Chapter 15

Orban's cannon

Figure 15.1: Cannon warfare. Image courtesy of Steve Estvanik.

My name is Orban. No relation to Prince Orhan or Orkan or any other 'Or' for that matter.

I am technically known as a Hungarian, though I am from Transylvania and I make cannons; I was schooled as an engineer and I understand the velocity of military war machines such as the cannon.

Last year, I offered my services to Constantinople. I travelled all the way to meet the emperor. I could build him a gigantic cannon that would scare the enemy and batter their numbers. Christianity would be saved! Alas, he could not afford my exorbitant salary. Hey, I do not come cheap for my expertise. Besides, I could tell that CONstantine would not have afforded the resources that go into CONstructing the weapon of mass destructiveness.

I guess I took off, unable to convince them, and approached the Ottoman leader who was preparing his siege.

"I can blast the walls of Babylon itself", I boasted. Sure enough this young man did not haggle like the emperor, he provided me with the coins and gold I needed to whet my appetite. I would be a very wealthy man for the rest of my life. WEALTHY! An easy life ahead for me, kudos to me.

I also had access to gunpowder, the first time it would be used with such cannon blasts, or at least this is what I told the sultan. I certainly was not aware of anyone else utilising gunpowder in this way. Perhaps you can also call me a pioneer, not just an engineer.

With a few assistants I built a large gun within three months at Adrianople. In March, the gun and some smaller ones were dragged by sixty oxen to the city. I cannot or *cannon* wait to see the look on the face of the emperor when the giant gun starts on the walls of his city. *Hey man, I did try to offer you my services!*

Drawback? Takes hours to reload and requires many men to accomplish the task. Any large cannon will need stone masons to help create a stabilising foundation to ensure the contraption remains static after the blast. The upside? A large cannon such as the one created by me will cause significant damage and stress to any stone wall. I know my craft and having spent time living in a walled city during my youth, I also understood the strength behind the medieval wall.

Chapter 16

Venice, the pope, some Russians and a cardinal—no, they all didn't walk into a bar

I remember sitting in Saint Mark's Square in Venice, admiring what was in front me. Such an intriguing city, this was the place to be. There was a gala, lots of colour, people enjoying themselves and the canals.

With this context in mind, many people will be unaware of the Greek speaking influence in Venice. As I strolled around Venice, you could feel the history and the splendour of Venice. However, if you blinked you would miss the Greek connection. In fact, I was in Venice to represent the emperor, not to holiday and it was by chance that I stumbled upon a Greek church. I remember how excited the Venetian couple standing in front of me became when I explained I could speak Greek. “Gei sou, I am George, do you speak any Greek?”

Venice was founded in 421 AD as tradition tells us or in the 600s, when the small communes banded together as one community under a leader called the Doge. Most of Italy during that epoch was under the control of Constantinople with the south being notable for the use of Greek as the lingua franca.

An early and important Doge was Orso Ipato, a Greek who was born in Heraclea in Calabria. The Doge had to report to the emperor, however, Venice was in essence an independent state whose foreign relations and some taxes were controlled by Constantinople. In 810, the Holy Roman Empire made an unsuccessful attempt to capture Venice, resulting in a treaty that recognised the authority of Constantinople.

Despite the treaty that was signed a year later, it is probable that this is the period when our control of Venice was essentially at an end. For our military had to contend with the Bulgars, Slavs, Saracens and Avars who were entering the empire from the east and north. Venice could be let go as a distant territory. Unfortunately, this was one decision that would ultimately prove disastrous when you consider the disgraceful act of looting Constantinople in 1204/5 and the rise of Venice as a rival power. Two factors that had far reaching consequences on history for Europe and indeed my people.

In 1082, the emperor Alexios Komnenos signed a Treaty with Venice which guaranteed them extensive trade and commerce in Byzantium, in return for their military support against the 'barbaric' dogs we know as the Normans. The newfound trade opportunities allowed Venice to grow into the great power they have become within a century.

Over the last few decades, many Greek speakers have migrated to Venice for protection against the Ottomans. There are possibly thousands of Greek speakers or descendants in Venice, and I understand a Greek library is being built pronto.

They always say about Greek and Italian relations, *una fatsa, una ratsa,* which means one face, one race in Latin. This has traditionally referred to the Greek people in Calabria, Apulia, Sicilia and Sardinia, not Venice.

Anyway, I digress a little. Remember, I, Sphrantzes, am a chronicler as well as an ambassador for the emperor. I was here to convince the Venetians that they should help us in the fight ahead.

I addressed the Doge. I addressed the senate. An appeal was also sent to the Vatican. I appealed to our shared sense of history, how the Greek speakers had provided a strong influence in Venice. I then argued about the disruption of commerce, the looming threat to the republics, and how we had held out these barbarians for centuries as the Venetians grew from skinny children to fat adults on the back of our front-line resistance.

⋆ ⋆

What can one say about a leader of a massive religion, particularly the leader who represents the Christians in the West? At this juncture in time, the pope had a lot on his blessed silver plate, which I will explain in a moment.

Once, our churches were united. Some of the early men who became pope, were of Greek stock in Italy. These last few centuries have unbound our connectedness on a number of theological and political viewpoints. This had a detrimental effect on the Greek speakers dealing with invaders from faraway lands into Europe. The biggest bone of contention is filioque and who should technically lead Christianity. I always thought Jesus or God would be good enough, but no, it is either the pope or the patriarch.

Sure, the pope is not a warrior, he is a diplomat. And a diplomat can make significant errors of judgement when his cup is overflowing.

Pope Nicholas V has been in place now for six years. In that time, he has insisted that Greek speakers come under his papacy or there will be no support against barbarians or Saracens. The looming crisis against the Ottomans could only be settled by forcing Constantinople under his leadership. Nicholas has also had to deal with the French and English in the winding down of the Hundred Years War. Idiots. They could have been at Constantinople fighting the invaders. Nicholas was also busy with plans for the Saint Peter Basilica and accepting refugees from Greek speaking lands; and there was the matter of intervening in the issue between Spain and Portugal of the Gran Canarias.

Then, he had to deal with the Portuguese slave trade. This may have troubled him at night, for it is claimed that he slept poorly at times. Having expanded into western Africa in recent years, Portuguese merchants realised that with superior military equipment, they may be able to make significant wealth from poor wretched souls, whose only crime was to be at the wrong place at the worst possible time. For these *God-fearing* Christians, the economic element of slave trafficking is immense. A greedy captain named Antam Gonçalvez, probably accelerated the 'industry' when his men kidnapped up to six Berbers not long before Nicholas became pope.

Prince Henry of Portugal was pleased to hear the news. Money, power, happy citizenry and not offending the pope, what a windfall? Instead of helping their fellow Christians in Constantinople, they were of course busy....

The Berbers managed to convince Gonçalves that if they were freed, they would return to Africa and capture ten sub-Saharan Africans with Portuguese help in exchange for freedom. The pope, in his wisdom, rather than condemn the slave trade, he simply released a Papal bull that allowed for the slave trade of persons who are not Christian, Jewish or Muslims. Essentially persons who were black.

Oh, I am often told by representatives of the pope, he provided this overt support for slavery on the basis that the Portuguese would help fight the Ottomans. Yes indeed, a small number arrived in Italy, and then never joined any rescue mission.

Clearly, we had a genius sultan to deal with and a pope with way too much to juggle. Not good omens for us.

⋆⋆

As someone who became a big patron of the arts, and also restored cleansing and beautification to Rome, the pope wanted to support the Greeks, even if it were on his terms. He admired the artisans that existed in Greek history.

He ordered and paid for ten ships to join a predominantly Venetian fleet, hoping that it would be augmented by Genoa and the Greek established Napoli. This was commissioned almost a year before the sultan showed up to our gates. Additionally sending an ambassador to reason with the Venetians to send a fleet and resources to Constantinople.

Around the same time as the ten ships were ordered, the pope held discussions with 'his' trusty cardinal, Isodore.

The cardinal was born in the Morea, following a divine path to Constantinople to become a monk at the monastery of Saint Demetrius. He was one of the Greeks who knew Latin fluently and was well known as an orator, theologian and for the reunification of the two Christian churches. The emperor John Palaeologus appointed him to the position of Metropolitan of Kiev and all Rus' to bring that part of the world into the murky folds of union. He was not well disposed of by the leader of the Rus, Vasilli II and aside from being held against his will in a small room and escaping at one point, there was no real love for a union. The Rus understood the enormity of supporting the emperor. They did not look favourably upon Latin people for reasons of religious differences and for their betrayal of Constantinople in the past. As it was the Greeks who had converted them 500 years earlier, they had a feeling of loyalty to Constantinople.

Anyway, again I am digressing from the main point. The pope before Nicholas, Eugene IV, anointed him the legate for all Ruthenia and Lithuania, and cardinal-priest, Saint Peter and Saint Marcellinus, despite being nominally under the church of Constantinople.

At some stage before the end of 1443, he returned to Rome after an expedition across the coldest parts of Europe, escaping from the disgruntled clergy of Moscow. Nicholas tasked him with arranging the reunion of the churches at Hagia Sofia. He brought with him 200 soldiers, mostly archers, from the pope. This last element was a welcome gift. The reunion of churches was not welcomed by the average citizen. We, the average citizen, felt he would bring the wrath of God down upon us.

⋆⋆

Meanwhile, there was a monk who was looked upon for direction by many of his colleagues and the average citizenry; Gennadius, who watched in disbelief. He originally supported reunion as the price to pay for help. Upon a looooong reflection, he promptly changed his mind and was promptly dispatched to a form of exile in the city, fearing too that God would not approve of the union. Would history prove him to be correct?

Chapter 17

Heraclius and Basil Flashback

The empire was not always this fragmented and small. I am Heraclius, and I am an emperor of great military skill, God's representative on earth and the one who regained the true cross of Jesus when I reconquered Jerusalem in 602 from our fierce enemy, the Sassanids (Persian). I ended any pretension of the empire not being Greek through a series of cultural reforms including recognising the language of the people, Greek, as the language of the administration. Before my reign there was a mixed bag of Latin, Greek and Armenian men and women who led the empire.

A mysterious warrior, a brave and legendary warrior, once sent me a note when I was on campaign in Asia. He wrote to tell me that I should adhere to his God, Allah. This was an audacious letter. I did not reply. Though I did keep the letter and took it back with me to Constantinople after my campaign in Asia.

At the end of my reign, this superpower of the medieval world was beginning to see a decline, with our territory shrinking across the Mediterranean, especially the African provinces that were lost to inspired Arab soldiers who swept through over a period of a few short decades. The sender of the letter had inspired fighters and people to join his faith. His name was Muhammad, born of Mecca and revered to his people as a prophet.

For the record, the last African outpost was lost in 711 AD at Septum, opposite Spain. We were stretched somewhat as an empire, and I can tell you the loss of Egypt meant we needed to locate quality and cheap wheat from elsewhere. This was a loss that was hard to fathom.

⋆⋆

My name is Basil II (976–1025), from the Macedonian Dynasty. The first Basil from almost a century prior initiated a series of reforms that re-ignited the economy, reclaimed numerous Greek dominated areas, such as Magna Graecia in Italy and the Crimea in the Black Sea. The House of Macedon is from a region or *theme* as we call it, in what some call Thrace, not the ancient Greek kingdom of Makedonia.

By the time I came to the throne, the empire was flourishing as a place of learning especially in Constantinople, known for its arts scene and in particular the mosaics inside churches and the painting of icons, the impressive architecture of churches and public buildings as well as the strength of its economy. Our currency, "nomisma" was the currency across the known world. It was during these times that a new style of governing was developed and that continues today. Constantinople was the home of many public departments, which unlike the feudal system in Latin Europe, citizens were essentially running the day-to-day affairs of the empire through a bureaucracy.

I ensured that the empire stretched across half of the Mediterranean including Magna Graecia, Palestine and Judea, most of the Black Sea and territory up to the Danube. Only the stupidity of

Greeks could harm our great empire. If I were a future emperor 150 years later, and I say my name is Romanus and I am fighting the Seljuk Turkish nomads just inside Syria at Manzikert, I would not be overly confident. I would not rush into a battle. Always try diplomacy first with barbarians and then outthink them if you are in battle. Fight a battle in favourable conditions and let me say if I were at Manzikert years from now, I would not want to lose, for the Turkmen will consequently make gains in Anatolia every few decades thereafter. If that ever did happen in the distant future, people would scream, "Oh Romanus, what happened that day, that fateful day that changed the course of history? How did you fuck it up?"

Chapter 18

A tough attack

Back in the present, the sultan had felt that the bombardment was going to plan. It was time for Zaganos and the sultan to test the resilience of the defenders. Both had been satisfied with strength of the military.

"General, how many people do you think we have as fighters, infantry, cavalry and Janissaries, as well as support personnel and our navy?" He asked his commander.

"My sultan, I can tell you the emperor can count his force almost by hand within the day, we would need a week or more to make a count! By your good grace, we will have a pool of 200,000 people including non-military, though we do have a good minority; the irregulars who are not well endowed with body armour or weaponry."

Satisfied, the sultan nodded.

I, Sphrantzes could indeed count the opposition in a day. Possibly on one hand! When the emperor asked me to make a count just days before the gates of the city were locked and bridges leading in were destroyed, the count revealed almost 8,000. Most of them were of Greek origin, be it Constantinople, or somewhere in the

Figure 18.1: Theodosius walls. Image courtesy of Hayirhah.

Greek East. I had hoped Cyprus would send support. We had been waiting on Venice. Would Theodora arrive in time to alert the King at Trebizond. What about the Morea to send troops, I know Persephone, she will be pushing the despots. Magna Graecia. Hungary. Genoa. Kiev. Disaffected Arabs. Georgia. The Principality of Theodoro. Crete. Alexandria with a minority Greek population despite it being under the Mamelukes. Emperor Manuel had once begged the English and the French. If the city could hold out and just a quarter of these turn up, Constantinople would be saved. People in the city believed the Holy Virgin would protect them, just as the sultan looked to Allah. When it came down to it, this would be a battle of bodies and resources. Ours of course are limited.

Against these bare bone defenders, the sultan had a huge military. Zaganos and the commanders would have no problem losing soldiers to test the defence.

On 18 April, he was allowed to let loose.

⋆⋆

My name is Zaganos Pasha, and I want to tell you something. I was born a Christian in Northern Epiros. I was subject to the system of Devşirme, when I was taken as a young boy and converted. I embraced my new culture and climbed the ranks of the Janissary until I was a commander and the first ever vizier who was born a Christian. I have no love for Hilal. He may as well have been born a Greek; he probably takes their gold. I know that he sends the emperor secret messages. When we take the city soon, I will deal with him for he feigns conservative tactics in our Council meeting. I simply believe he wants to undermine the sultan. My loyalty is to the sultan. People who do not follow, do not need to remain in our orbit. Halil, take your gold and go to hell.

My best fighter is Ulubatlı Hasan and I expect this man mountain to destroy many of the enemy. I also have under my command sappers. These are the people who will tunnel underground, many were recruited from Germania. They are quick and skilful, and I hope to either weaken the towers by tunnelling underneath or send as many of my troops under the defenders to surprise them.

He has taken my advice and stretched the European troops, across the length of the walls. He has chosen Karadja Pasha to lead them overall.

The regulars from Anatolia have been assigned Ishak Pasha, and they are positioned to the south of the Lycus toward the Marmara.

Orban, his cannon, the sultan and the Janissaries are facing what we expect is the weaker Saint Romanos Gate, around the Mesoteichion. The gate being named after an emperor who failed us at Manzikert, for he was no Basil, was he?

The irregulars are filtered across all of these. They were here for the gold, loot, pillaging and rape. For they are not paid soldiers.

My own direct troops will be stationed to the north of the Golden Horn. Every day I would be at the side of the sultan for strategy and support.

Overall, the best way is to overpower the defenders by systematically chipping at the walls from the front and underground, using our huge numbers to wear them down if a breech opens up. That is why I like the irregulars, I may not break bread with these people, but they were simple enough to expend. Useful.

⋆ ⋆

The Commanders were like bulls about to be released. We called in the irregulars and told them to sacrifice for the greater good. “If you succeed and climb the walls, you will be remembered for all eternity. You will have as much gold from the filthy heathen as you want. Go and show these immoral dogs what we are and who we are.....”

As the sun rose, the first group of irregular fighters ran as fast as they could. It was as if entry to the Greek only Olympic Games was the prize. Why these men thought that they could scale stone and brick walls that reached the height of almost nine metres for the outer and 12 metres for inner, five metres in diameter for the outer, topped by 96 towers that reached 20 meters above ground, is anyone's guess. The well protected towers with archers in abundance. These attackers of course with minimal skill of climbing straight walls in a siege may also have suffered from the symptoms of vertigo. They truly were lambs to the slaughter.

One by one Giustiniani's men picked off the hapless visitors. The Genoans and the Chiotes in his regiment took bets with a Scotsman named Grant to see who could take the most men. The cardinal's archers declined to bet out of respect to their religion; they succeeded in clearing the walls. By the end of the day, hundreds of the Bashi-bazouk were lifeless in the ditches below. Some of these ditches were a few metres deep and 20 metres wide. An ideal location for expendable fighters.

Giustiniani, aware that these men would show no mercy if they took the city, displayed his compassion. He allowed volunteers from the enemy camp to reclaim the fallen for burial. In the mind of the emperor, a sensible decision as it would show the enemy camp the full effect of a bad day for the campaign. It would also rid the ditches of corpses that could decay and wreak, unless you were a defender without a sense of smell.

We, in turn, appreciated the unplanned goodwill of the defenders by wanting to bring them down. I am sure it was hoped that this goodwill could be remembered when the city falls, unless of course amnesia sets in for us. And amnesia was not uncommon amongst blood thirsty fighters.

⋆⋆

Constantinople had a series of small and military (larger) gates, with the keys entrusted to a select few of nobility, Giustiniani and the priest who resided on the lower level of the Blachernae Palace.

The Emperor, always thinking and willing to explore was having a quick counsel with Sphrantzes, the priest, Lukas Notaras, Giustiniani and Grant the Scot.

It was Grant who asked how good Giustiniani's men were at quick sorties. The Emperor's ears pricked up.

"I could bet you some of my whiskey that your men are not quick enough to maim or kidnap some of the enemy who venture dangerously close to the ditches."

Giustiniani, taking the bait, "quicker than a pasty white ginger tunnel engineer."

"How so?"

"I have the keys to some of the gates including the kerkoporta where the Bocchiardi brothers are based. That is where a couple of dozen men come to the ditches daily with their hilarious taunts. I am not sure if they realise that we only speak Latin or Greek!"

Interrupting, the emperor offered, "suppose that I lead out a small party today and Giustiniani tomorrow. We can see who the quickest team is, Greeks or Genoan and in the process pick off a few of their men."

"Are you mad Constantine?"

It was a chorus of Sphrantzes, the priest and Irene who was dropping off some meals prepared by the kitchen. The men were startled to see her; though Grant was pleased and immediately broke off from the others with an excuse about a vegetarian meal that he wanted prepared in order to talk to the *Goddess* in the room. Any excuse to speak to the smiling smartly dressed, similarly blushing, woman before him, even though he wasn't actually a vegetarian.

Leaving Grant to be a Casanova with his ethereal beauty, the rest of the table debated the merits of a gamble.

Joined now by an observing Venetian bailey, always the pragmatist, Sphrantzes made the obvious point that neither leader could ill afford to be captured and just the loss of one man, would be a big loss for the already stretched defences. “We are best sticking to our defence behind the walls. We need to be conservative here. . . .”

“My dear friend secretary, this is what I do. It almost worked at Hexamilion and it has worked elsewhere.” The emperor interrupted a clearly distraught Sphrantzes, who thought it best to let the Bocchiardi brothers undertake a daring task instead.

The next morning, as the chill of the evening made way for a cloudless and sunny day, one that invited a gathering of eagles, the emperor acceded to Sphrantzes’ demand that he at least take off his purple regalia to avoid being an obvious target.

His standard bearer ignored the warning not to draw attention with an imperial looking outfit; much to his detriment as he was easily cut down when the emperor and a group of 20 came riding out of the gate.

As he had expected, a similar number of enemy were quickly beaten and mopped up, with the loss of just the standard bearer. It was almost like watching a blues vs green contest at the Hippodrome in its prime, as hundreds of faithful watched from the safety of the high walls. The emperor had accomplished his mission in less than nine minutes.

The next day, Giustiniani attempted the same routine. With a bigger group this time including the Bocchiardi, the Genoan rode a little further out as the enemy kept a greater distance for their daily taunting. None of these taunters were an obstacle to the Genoan. With a boisterous crowd behind him and a large contingent of the sultan’s regulars running to the aid of their fallen soldiers, Giustiniani’s men made light work of their task in eight minutes. Each adversary would meet the blade of the attackers, their horses gave the height advantage to be able to batter each attempted defensive block from the soon to be victim. And for those of the enemy who did not fall to a sword, a spear was the next best friend for the Bocchiardi, who returned with a few prisoners, and one casualty.

"This madness ends now." It was an angry Venetian bailey. "No more sorties, two dead is bad for business. We need people alive and on the walls. We simply have too few. I cannot allow anyone else to be risked for your sadistic fun. We win by keeping our numbers and then I can go back to commercial activity."

⋆⋆

Both the emperor and Giustiniani shrugged off the valid criticism. Both agreed to the request of the Venetian who was now also joined by an unhappy imperial secretary. The Bocchiardi brothers quickly disappeared, for they were not keen on conservative actions, or direction by a Venetian.

"Anyone seen Grant? Is he still trying to become a dad or husband?" It was Giustiniani in need of some of the Scottish brew that was promised if the Genoan won.

"I can report, he is making slow progress on that first task. He is also having a look at our underground tunnels and listening out for possible mining activity. Our spies in their camp tell us that they have shipped in a number of engineers from Egypt and Germania for possible mining under our walls. It is probably a lie, however, we will need to keep on top of that, literally," Sphrantzes reported solemnly.

Chapter 19

The attack of the Serbians

Mehmed watched as a band of irregulars joined by Serbians made the initial effort to attack. The Serbs ran as fast as they could. On this day, they could have beaten any given horse. The 200 Serbians were just a small component of the Serbian contingent.

Why they would create a suicide mission was beyond Hasan who wanted to be running out there with them. He scratched his head as he watched from a distance. "Are these idiots just fools or suicidal? The irregulars should go first," he spoke with a baritone voice to match his size, speaking to a smaller fighter next to him, who looked at what was blocking the sun!

The front runner paused near the wall and pulled out a white cloth. It may have had the image of an eagle on it.

"Hurry, we are defecting to the emperor by the grace of God," the front runner yelled.

The emperor, without hesitation or looking at the surprised Notaras for his reaction, ordered, "throw ropes to the Serbians and welcome them to Constantinople. Ensure they surrender their weapons for the time being and take them to sit with our reserve infantry. I will join my fellow people for a briefing later."

The enemy camp looked on, disbelieving that anyone could change sides. Yet the Serbs had come here under duress, and while many were indeed fighting for the sultan to preserve the safety of their homeland, this brave bunch could not fathom fighting for anyone other than a Christian who was of a similar bloodline thanks to Helena Dragases.

⋆⋆

The irregulars who were also caught off guard were soon easy fodder for the Greek Fire used by the determined defenders. A special liquid that was the city's equivalent of a Hungarian cannon, or perhaps a fire breathing dragon in its effect.

Over at the Kerkoporta, a black steel gate, the Bocchiardi brothers were pleased to see action. Despite orders not to, they ventured out from the gate and fought the Ottomans. The irregulars were no match for these spirited soldiers, dressed in the latest chain mail and riding the finest horses that Thrace had seen. These 'fools' would undertake this form of attacking madness more times before the siege was finished.

This small attack in the early days of the campaign proved to be more of a prod and test the water initiative, to see how the emperor could cope after heavy bombardment.

If this were a school test, the emperor would be the dux of the class as they sailed through with the ease befitting a well-prepared defence.

Chapter 20

From Prince Orhan to the engineer Orban

From the outset, I am no real fan of the Greeks. They keep me in Constantinople as a 'prisoner.' I admit, I have luxurious quarters that overlook the Bosporus. I was not happy when I was initially housed facing Thrace, too many little towns and greenery. I prefer the calm of the water in my new abode, the serene harbour of Eptaskalio. In the distance I can see my beautiful Asia, *my empire.*

My name is Orhan Çelebi, I'm a 41-year-old with almost 700 men at my disposal. Good Muslim men who stay in my neighbourhood, as we generally stick together, though we are neither at war with the Greeks or Italians, nor are we their best friends. The city has a mosque, then again it has several Catholic churches too and a place of worship for Armenians and for Jews, as it is a city of tolerance to the foreigner. Oh, my uncle was Mehmed I.

As for my 'imprisonment,' well, I am a good income generator for the emperor and an insurance policy. You see, I was a rival to the Sultancy. I have the bloodline inherently flowing through me. If I venture into Asia or any Ottoman province, I may not have enough men to defeat the sultan, but I could raise a rebellion. Constantine keeps me here at the expense of the sultan. Yes, you heard me correct. He pays for me to be held here in order to prevent me from fermenting revolt. Constantinople has hosted many hostages like me, in the past. To be fair, we are allowed our freedom and essentially left to our own customs. Sphrantzes visits me from time to time and the emperor has taken my advice about the 21-year-old sultan, who now threatens this city. We will fight to protect my honour, and all those of my bloodline that Mehmed has wronged. If we win, I will march on the Ottoman empire for the young sultan will be mortally wounded. I know I can turn the Janissary, who are loyal to the rules, but not entirely sold on this young upstart.

We are ready, we are trained, and we are praying five times a day.

Come what may, and it will be May soon enough, we will be ready for my cousin.

⋆⋆

While I, Orhan, am no relation to Orban the engineer, it is interesting that I may have had a lasting influence on the life of the Hungarian Orban.

One day, he set about organising a reload of the cannon, there had appeared to be a crack in the cannon. After informing Mehmed, he was forced by the commanders to make hasty repairs. Orban needed at least another day or two with the repairs. However, siege warfare waits for no one.

After reloading the cannon, Orban and his team prepared to lob a cannon ball. He wanted to slow down the reload, alas the sultan wanted a result.

On this day, the sultan had been thinking about how sweet it would be to do away with *Prince Orhan* by blasting these walls and finding his *stupid cousin,* teaching me a lesson.

"Ready men, steady please. The sultan is watching on."

These may have been the last words the Hungarian uttered as the cannon then, comically, self-exploded. It was an ironic way for the engineer to end his campaign, there would be no easy life ahead for this dead engineer.

On a rampart opposite, I had been watching. I smiled.

Chapter 21

Better the turban of the sultan, than that of the papa?

"It's better the turban of the sultan, than that of the papa (pope)," yelled a woman dressed all in black, mourning the loss of her husband. She yelled at the cardinal, a cardinal who was born Greek, had managed to be captured in Kiev and escaped. Here trapped by the Sultan, there was no escaping the wrath of the widow. She was angry, with her veins almost popping out of her the little bit of skin that could be discerned through the black outfit of mourning she wore.

Cardinal Isodore, a resident since the previous year, embarrassed, managed to get away to connect with his archers. He screams still ringing in his pointy ears. The 200 archers were supplied by Pope Nicholas. Yes, with the most important city to Christendom outside of Rome under threat, he 'wisely' sent a meagre 200 archers, in addition to sending his bishops to the Venetian senate to argue for a relieving fleet to be sent to aid Constantine.

The sacred position of pope had been filled many times by Greek speakers during the era when the Roman empire was one, under the rule of Constantinople.

Sadly, that precious link was not one to dwell upon.

“Why is there is such animosity to the cardinal?” Grant asked of Irene.

“My dear Scot in a kilt, you do look cute when you ask these innocent questions.”

“Are you trying to make me blush lassy?”

Smiling, she continued, “there was a schism four hundred years when the representatives of the pope left a papal bull of excommunication at Agia Sophia. The Crusaders who came to our shores with the blessing of the pope generally proved a nuisance, the Latins desecrated Constantinople and the Italian republics made gains at the expense of Constantinople, all the while we fought the new enemy from the east, a different religion.”

“Ayyyy,” Grant was able to muster.

“Then in 1439 at the Council of Florence, the eastern and western churches agreed to a union. Many of the signees from the clergy of Constantinople quickly repudiated the agreement as it ceded too much to the Vatican. Remember, the patriarch was considered a higher office than pope. As the empire grew weaker and the west broke away, the pope grew in power and stature. We also have the differences in filioque.”

Grant continued to nod and scratch his scruffy beard. Some lice fell out, which neither perturbed nor hindered him.

“Now they want us to recognise the decision of Florence or they will refrain from dispatching any more support. The Emperor has already recognised Florence in Mystra and again when the cardinal turned up. That is why most Greeks have not been attending Agia Sofia, the grand church, for service as the pope and their version of Christianity are being VENERATED! This is not ideal for us.”

"Oh dear. What ever happened to simply having a range of Gods to choose from on any given day with that Zeus guy leading the way as the boss? Just seems too complicated to me. Hating someone over religion. From what I know of the Latins and the Greeks, there are many similarities. I am surprised they cannot see that. If Venice thinks that the sultan won't come after their provinces, then they ought to stop drinking Greko Galliciano wine!" Grant retorted with a grim expression, having stopped scratching his scruffy beard, just as an eagle swooped low over the couple.

They do say that a bird that poops on a human receives good luck. The Eagle may have had constipation. Luck was not what the eagle was providing. It did however provide a thought for Grant.

"My beautiful, beautiful dear. We may never have the same freedom as the eagle again if the Latins don't arrive. I think just to be sure; we should get married. . . ."

"Grant, in my city, you can only marry if you are a virgin! That you are clearly not," she said laughing playfully. You are more like a ginger devil. I can marry you on maybe one condition.

"Anything, name it my dear."

"You get us out of this mess and to the safety of the looooong winters of Scotland."

He smiled. The eagle landed nearby.

Chapter 22

Baltoghlu on dangerous seas

It's not every day that I take pity on an enemy combatant. Alas, I am a chronicler as well as being the secretary for Constantine.

An adversary and possibly the only one I have sympathy for is Süleyman Baltaoğlu, the admiral of the fleet. I am unsure of how he rose up the ranks and if he is of Mongol extraction or Greek.

Baltoghlu commanded his fleet stationed at Diplokionion, which is on the European side of the Bosporus and known to us as the double pillars.

As a chronicler, I can honestly say that the admiral brought together 31 warships and 100 smaller vessels and transports in an orderly fashion. These were made up mostly of biremes, where two banks of rowers were sat on opposite sides and triremes. The latter were extensively utilised by ancient Greeks.

The siege strategy of the admiral was very straightforward. Blockade Constantinople from every angle at sea and look out for any relieving fleets from elsewhere. The admiral had built up the fleet and recruited the men required. Remember, the Turk is not a seafaring person, the Greeks of course are, thus many a Christian was recruited as a rower or for other tasks on board the fleet.

The admiral had also succeeded in keeping any vessels from leaving the Morea, though, truth be told, I think they would have lost to the Greeks if Demetrios and Thomas had bothered to challenge them. In fact the Venetians and Genoans, with their experience, could beat the Ottoman fleet in an open sea engagement with far less ships. This is just the way it is.

Until this point, the admiral had done all that was asked of him, earning the respect of his fleet. He ate with the sailors, motivated them, mentored and encouraged as many of the crew as he could.

A week after Orban had fired his great cannon, the admiral attempted to take the chain connecting Galata and Constantinople. It is with immense pride that the limited forces of the emperor held the line and counter attacked.

The fleet did succeed in taking the nine islands that comprise the Prince's islands in the Sea of Marmara. Though almost all the population had already withdrawn behind the walls of Constantinople. The islands have a number of our churches and the Big Island convent. The latter was once home of exile for a range of empresses including Irene, Euphrosyne, Theophano, Zoe and Anna Dalassena.

Why the sultan thought that his fleet was a match for us at sea is one of life's mysteries. What tipped the sultan from an amicable relationship with his admiral was one of the best moments of my life, when a David and Goliath episode emerged. Four ships that appeared from the direction of the Aegean against the entire fleet; another form of theatre and sport that would have been ideally suited to the Hippodrome.

Three relief ships from the pope and one large imperial vessel. After sending an emissary to Venice and having had a guarantee that the Greeks would adhere to the Vatican version of Christianity, three boats were immediately dispatched. Each contained supplies, weapons, defenders and bibles. Not sure about Holy Water though.

The small flotilla had sailed almost smoothly past the region of Gallipoli. They had no intention of disembarking and climbing hills there, when they could easily sail to the city and disembark in the harbour. The flotilla had sailed passed as if they were cruising the Greek islands for a holiday rather than through a hostile environment.

The entire fleet may have been asleep, sometimes even the most energetic seamen can daydream. With a nice breeze behind them, they were just about to reach the Golden Horn where the chain would be detached to allow them through.

High up in the towers, Constantine and Giustiniani and what appeared to be the whole city were wide awake, for it was lunch time. Everyone was willing the flotilla on. Immense pride and joy could be felt. To those watching, this was a precursor for the Venetian fleet that would arrive to rescue the city; 1204 would soon be forgiven.

Grant took bets and suggested to Irene that the Greek boat would win the race. . . .

And then it happened. Just like a theatre production of an ancient Greek tragedy, there was high drama and a twist to come. The wind dropped and the enemy by this stage had awoken from their slumber.

Baltaoglu summoned dozens of vessels for a call to action, himself leading a boat as the crew rowed frantically. He was not about to let the watching sultan down. A sultan who had shown tremendous faith in the admiral.

By now, the four vessels were drifting back toward the Ottoman fleet, to the horror of the watching crowd in the city and the delight of the Ottoman military who were cheering from the shore. Now it did appear that the Hippodrome arena had made its way to the sea.

The European warships against the Asian. The pope had sent tall galleys and the Greek vessel was of similar stature. They backed into each other to limit entry points for the Ottomans and make it easy to fight, for these ships were in no mood to surrender to barbarians. No surrender!

Above them circled a group of eagles, part of the insignia of the emperor. A true omen for any sailor.

One by one the boats were destroyed by the superior Italian counterparts. Small cannons that were expertly used and expertise in sea fighting gave the four boats an advantage.

The admiral was wounded trying to board the Greek vessel. He tried to fight on. Casualties on the enemy's side were likely to have been in the high hundreds as Greek Fire from the imperial vessel wrought destruction. The admiral pressed on.

Mehmed was knee deep in water urging the fleet on from the safety of the European shore. Why didn't he join them? Unlike King Xerxes who whipped the Bosporus when he lost ships crossing over to Byzantium almost 2000 years ago, he was going to whip his admiral instead of the water, if he failed.

The allied boats were relentless at beating off each one of the attempted invaders. Swords, cannon, spears, knives and possibly holy water, all came to the aid of the defenders.

And then it happened again. The eagles took flight as a high wind picked up again catching the sails of jubilant European sailors who breezed past a temporary loosened chain in the Golden Horn. They were too fast and too competent for the attempted, lethargic chasers. The cheering that was heard in the city and Galata was the equivalent of any roar that the Hippodrome had ever experienced.

The sultan knew that this could be the advance force of a rescue fleet from Venice. Seething, he ordered the execution of Baltaoglu. He was beyond enraged and humiliated. Luck had deserted him, and his fleet displayed the weakness of a fledgling element of his military. Luck however was on hand to save the admiral as his sailors stepped in to explain that the admiral had fought as best as he could. He did not shirk his duties despite being wounded in the fighting. Moved that these men could stand up for a humiliated admiral in a time of crushing defeat, he allowed him to live. He was immediately stripped of his rank and banished to exile and poverty.

I never heard of Baltoghlu again in my life. As a chronicler, it would be ideal to have that information. If he were smarter, he could have come over to us, in a similar way that Alcibiades did during the Peloponnesian war, going from the Athenians to the Spartans during the Sicilian expedition.

Chapter 23

Another way to attack

"We have had mixed results. The area around Constantinople in Europe and Asia is ours, we control the sea except for the Golden Horn. Some of the walls are showing considerable damage. The arrival of the papacy boats are not a good omen. I want to send a message to the emperor; I want to show that we fear no one except Allah." It was the sultan, sitting around his tent, talking tactics to his viziers and Commanders. He was calm and serene. He kept visualising Constantinople being taken.

"Attack!" Came a quick reply from Zaganos.

Mehmed, was quick to concur, nodded. "Tomorrow, I want to test their mental readiness and energy. Every night citizens repair the walls and defenders go to sleep. Tomorrow night we will keep them awake for a few hours. Unless they are insomniacs."

Continuing, "unlike the effort a few days ago, this will be a proper attack that will take up a portion of the night. In the morning, I want our cannons to fire relentlessly to see if we can damage the unrepaired sections."

The viziers agreed in unison before finishing their tsai.

Zaganos was already out of the tent and on his way to inform fellow commanders of the plan. He will be on the front line again urging the non-regulars. “Those poor dim idiots, they will have no chance, but we need their sacrifice,” he mumbled to himself as walked briskly to his black and white horse that patiently waited for its rider.

⋆⋆

In Constantinople, as a warm day soon gave way to an evening chill, weary defenders were preparing to visit their family homes. Mostly women, elderly and priests took their place every night to help effect the repairs which were supervised by the indefatigable Giustiniani. It was fortunate that the Genoan was on duty as he quickly spotted what appeared to be a group of lunatics silently running toward the ditches. Giustiniani had no time to think. Sounding the alarm, he simultaneously sent runners through the streets to call back soldiers who had concluded their daily duty.

Church bells commenced a frantic round of ringing.

Notwithstanding the sentries that were on duty every evening for such an event, an evening attack by and large went against the conventional norm of battles and siege warfare.

The emperor, God’s representative on earth came dashing from a church and onto his horse. His purple regalia and flapping cape provided him with an air of invincibility. People saluted and applauded him as he rode at breakneck speed to Giustiniani, just in time for the Genoan to welcome him with a smile.

“Constantine, they are sending in their irregulars. Those brainless half-breed fools. Like donkeys to the slaughter.”

“What have we prepared for the donkeys?” Grinned a satisfied emperor.

“Lukas is readying for the Greek Fire. We thought we could toy with them a while to practise some archery and stone pelting.”

Unusually, while on duty, the emperor broke into a wry smile. “I, seriously, pity the fools.”

After what seemed like an hour of easy pickings, Notaras signalled men and women all along the ramparts to unleash the Greek Fire. The well-guarded secret behind the Greek Fire means no enemy will ever know how it worked. I certainly will not tell you. Unlike other sieges around the world, which relied on grease or substances to that effect, the empire had perfected a weapon that would easily deal with anyone, especially those with cheap fabric for bodily protection.

Like a goldfish that forgets what occurred only moments early, hundreds more irregulars were sacrificed, possibly over a thousand with negligible losses from the city. The sultan would not miss these men, for they had served a purpose regardless and would be rewarded in the afterlife. With no chance of a breakthrough, the 'attack' was called off in the early hours of the morning.

The victorious defenders thanked the ultimate defender of their city and took a well-earned break.... Until the cannons began pounding the walls when it was light again.

⋆⋆

Notaras was observing all of this from the outer wall. He had been involved in a number of campaigns in his almost privileged life. Almost, in that nobility are usually at the top of tree, with the common people down below, somewhat like a pyramid of Egypt. The empire had declined to such an extent that nobility, priests, merchants and peasants were now all on the same level fighting for one common goal. He looked behind him and admired the resolve of priests and nuns to carry icons and pray. Chant. What were they chanting today? It gave the defenders a rhythm and blocked out the noise coming from over the walls. The trumpets and banging of drums were no match to these beautiful angelic voices.

"What would happen to these angelic voices if Constantinople is lost?" Asking his question out a loud. A nun who had come up to assist a group of children on repairs for the wall heard the question and replied in song. She sang about her saviour and then continued to chant.

As the chanting drifted into the calm of the night, it was replaced by a period of overnight rain and a breeze, and then something stirred in the distance.

Chapter 24

Quarrel, Italian style

The Italian states had grown powerful, chiefly at the expense of the empire. Venice had gained significant trade concessions during the reign of Alexius Komnenos in the eleventh century, some years after the debacle of Manzikert when Romanus stupidly engaged the Seljuks in unfavourable terrain.

The Venetians were granted a baily to look after their affairs and their own quarter. This was in response to the Venetians and other crusaders helping the empire regain lost cities, such as Antioch and part of Syria. The emperor had to fight to reclaim territory that the Normans did not want to return to the emperor in Asia Minor. The Normans were not exactly trustworthy people and many a battle was fought with the empire in Epiros, Magna Graecia and the Mediterranean. Some of the emperors fought with them in their respective heads, such was the mentally draining effect of the Normans. Adding to this list of 'enemies/friends' were the Bulgars who were annihilated a few years earlier by Basil II, before a recent resurgence, the Arabs in the Mediterranean and a string of illiterate idiots, pardon my French, from the West taking lands that belonged to us. Cyprus anyone?

Alexius, as the price to pay for a growing maritime power that was considered more civilised than the others, one that had been under the nominal control of Constantinople for a few centuries, was given trade concessions. These were significant and on favourable terms for Venice. Some years later the Genoans would attain similar, though less significant concessions. The Venetians truly rose as a maritime power thanks to the concessions, and every few decades they would take islands or territory that were Greek speaking. The Genoans similarly followed in their footsteps or windsails. That is a nasty way to say thank you for the boost they received from the empire.

Hence, the Venetians and Genoans, became the preeminent Italian powers, eclipsing Napoli, Pisa and others. There was a huge distrust amongst the two powers.

This distrust may have had some tragic consequences for the defence of the city. With the exception of Giustiniani, few Genoans were liked by the Venetians and vice versa.

The first two weeks of the siege was brutal. Not just due to the monster cannon and the constant cannon blast. These two groups constantly bickering and fighting each other. You would think these two groups were actually different religions, or worse still, Saracens or Turks.

It took Grant to come up with a novel way to bring peace.

⋆⋆

“Constantly arguing. These two groups bring dishonour to their places of origin,” stating the obvious to Irene and Sphrantzes. “In the Highlands, we would have it out and then go to the pub straight after.” Grant, scratching his head and adjusting his red and black kilt.

“Welcome to life as we now know it. They have grudges that go back centuries.” Irene replied.

"I wish these people could just cooperate better. We need them unified." Sphrantzes also stating the obvious over a glass of water as he looked out to a vast empty field. There were plenty of empty areas in the city.

"I tell ya what. Let me arrange for a fighting match. Their biggest brutes to slug it out, get it off their chests and others can join in. I will arrange a few bets too. We can call it the *final fight of champions.* They can hurl as many insults and then we all agree to go back to fighting the real enemy. As a gesture of goodwill, we can arrange that the losers of the best get a refund and the winners, well they can get a blessing from the cardinal and the promise of free wine from Lesvos when the siege is raised."

Everyone laughed at the absurdity of what Grant offered; as crazy as it sounded, especially to a partially deaf Sphrantzes, Grant was able to arrange a fight in a ring by the evening. Eight fighters partook in the action, four per side and a crowd of mostly Genoans, including from Galata who supplied a fighter, and Venetians, attended. The Emperor and Giustiniani declined to attend, preferring to tour the walls and assess logistics for the next day.

As a *brutish* fight was about to take place, Irene explained the rules including not to kill or maim your opponents across two rounds; it appeared that it was a good way to let out pent up steam and generate some laughter from the small, yet vocal crowd.

A few insults were traded. One side belittling the other about their achievements. All participants conscious not to mess hair or perfectly trimmed beards and eyebrows. Twenty minutes later and very little action had transpired, suffice to say a few more insults were traded over the respective outfits of each group. The Genoans preferred to wear the lighter colours they were accustomed to in their homeland and the Venetians, with access to superior silk and wool and designers, seemingly had more colourful designs.

These men wore a linen shirt with puffed out sleeves, a tight fitted doublet over the top, which would make it hard to breathe for those overweight. Each participant, having started their morning with an over robe.

Each man wore black breaches from the waist down to their leather shoes.

Genoa had a Magistrato delle Pompe, who enforced the fashion and style laws that regulated what citizenry could attire themselves in. Hence, they were not as well-matched clothing wise. Perhaps, the fashion on parade, the ability to insult using their tongue and hands and the necessity to keep hair styles secure ensured no punches were actually thrown.

Once all the verbal insults were traded, each side agreed to return to what mattered, saving Constantinople and trying to work collaboratively under immense pressure. Much to the disappointment of punters and the bemusement of Grant. Should they need to, Grant was rather willing to bring them back to any sparse field for a rumble or a yelling match. Most likely with the instruction next time not to wear their Sunday best.

Whether it was calculated to succeed or not, Grant had temporarily defused a festering rivalry just after a week since the real enemy had shown up.

⋆⋆

While Grant had come up with a creative way to deal with some of the Italians, another hurdle had to be dealt with in Venice, where another sparring area was set aside in the senate.

The senate, or rather the Consiglio dei Pregadi, was the body of deliberation for the Venetians. Notaras once remarked of the senate in jest on a visit to Sparta, "democracy at its finest, a proud moment for Cleisthenes or Pericles."

The emperor took the remark in a Laconian Spartan wit type of way; "the senate was made up of all the *finest people*. . . . Of noble stock only." Left to the people, many of whom had befriended

Greek refugees, and it's likely that the recalcitrant Venetian senate would have sent help much earlier, rather than dithering around.

There was a lively debate with a number of senators proclaiming that it best not to upset the sultan and simply let Constantinople fall. Others, with some gentle prompting from bishops sent by the pope, were able to point out both the daftness of allowing Constantinople to fall, risking the Venetian quarter and commerce and, of course, allowing people of similar culture to be enslaved. The Portuguese traders to Africa were already undertaking such savage trade, "we must show we are not of similar mindset. There will be no slaves, and none for the sultan." Came a call from one senator.

The previous August, senators, some would say delusional republicans, placed a motion to fellow senators to abandon Constantinople to its impending doom. The motion had been defeated. In November, Captain Rizzo and his crew were brought down by the 'Throat Cutter' of Rumeli Hisar, and more and more of Venetians became less complacent and in favour of assisting the city. For many in the senate, the idea of keeping their commercial interests had been prevalent from the outset. The pope would always lament that the common people enjoyed similar cultural traits as Constantinople. Unfortunately, the senate was driven by profit and they were already making good deals with the Ottoman representatives in Europe. The appalling Rizzo incident was the moment the gold coin dropped, and the lamp shed light on the dire situation of the Greeks, who were apparently of *similar cultura*.

When the senators finally voted early in the new year, it was on the basis that the expedition consisted of no more than 17 ships, most of them war galleys. The Venetian senate may have proven to be a costly delay for the people of Constantinople unless the fleet were to depart a few days after the sultan began his bombardment of the walls. A certain Alviso Longo was tasked with leading the fleet, with a significant instruction; that was to avoid confrontation unless drawn into a battle with the Sultan!

Similarly, Naples had been persuaded to send some support, which mysteriously did not make it to the Aegean. The pope had also managed a letter of warning from Frederick III of the Holy Roman Empire to send as an *empty threat* in March. The sultan likely added the letter to his daily toiletry supplies.

⋆⋆

In an attempt to gain some light relief and provide an evening of entertainment, a theatre performance was arranged. No one could quite remember what the play was about, it was a just an excuse for the emperor to bring representatives of all groups together. The comedy play was performed in Greek; it also contained words and phrases in various languages. Giustiniani smiled when he noticed a woman with a familiar smile. He had seen her perform before. Years ago in fact. He nodded and gently thanked her from his seat for the tour of the walls she had once provided. She did not see him. Suddenly his thoughts were all over the place. The smile, the warmth. His sub conscious had not forgotten. "No, this is not the time to be distracted." After being part of a standing ovation, he hurriedly scampered back the land walls, uncertain if the warm heart of an old flame had seen him. The Genoan needed to be true to his mind, not the heart.

Chapter 25

Return from Trebizond

It had been an unusually brutal ride along the Black Sea for this time of the year, with winds and heavy rain slowing the imperial boat. For Theodora, it had been three weeks of worry. She had a letter to deliver to King David and she was anxious about the fate of the city, and Constantine. She wanted to be there, not fleeing to Trebizond!

Granted, the emperor wanted Trebizond to send ships to Constantinople, as well as to keep her safe. He had already lost two wives in his lifetime. He didn't want to lose his next, future wife.

Three weeks at sea had felt like an eternity. Now, they could just make out the high walls of Trebizond in the distance, along the shore of the Pontus. The Pontus had been a special region for Greeks. The ancient colonies dated back over two thousand years. The region produced the brilliant, King Mithridates, who almost destroyed the power of Rome. Trebizond had prospered on the Silk Road and as a break away empire from Constantinople. The region was almost an island for her fellow Christians; well served by high walls and high mountains. Theodora, selfishly, wondered why the sultan couldn't just attack Trebizond and leave Constantinople alone. Though, any attempt would likely be met with aid from Georgia, ships from the Trebizond held part of Crimea, as well as the independent Principality of Theodoro, also in the Crimea. The latter is a Greek ruled province, next to the last remaining Crimean territory of Trebizond.

As the vessel kept inching towards the small speck on the horizon, her mind turned to another matter. A black pearl of a ship had sidled up next to the small imperial ship. The latter was essentially undermanned, or underwomanned as she had joked to the crew; consisting of several older Greek sailors, a number of women, two Arab traders caught up in the city who wanted to help in some way and teenage boys that the emperor wanted out of harm's way. They were all able enough to help row and work the ship. The vessel itself had always intended to return with any support King David could muster.

With about two days away from safety, pirates were an immediate impediment. Three planks were affixed to the side of the imperial vessel. Pirates seeking gold from an impoverished empire was always going to end in some form of disappoint.

Theodora knew what was at stake. The *captain* and Theodora tasked the elderly members of the crew to plank one and three. Theodora led the Arab merchants and the teenage boys to the second plank.

"On my call crew, on my call," she yelled. The crew readied as a rag tag group of ungroomed, dishevelled pirates began filing across the planks. As soon they were filled, the order was given.

The first and third planks heard a loud boom and witnessed a cloud of smoke. It was the their first and likely their last taste of Greek fire as the planks were replaced by an emptiness and bodies, which dropped into the sea; such an unforgiving and murky sea.

The pirates on the second plank, were spooked enough to be dealt with easily as they boarded the vessel. Those who survived and crossed over were *welcomed* as prisoners.

A total of nine survived and were bound and sent to the hull. A present for the King.

Theodora lost no time. She picked a small number of the crew and ushered them to the pirate ship, which contained several male and female slaves. The slaves, grateful at the rescue, were given an option of Trebizond or adventure. They chose the latter. Happy to see the end of the pirates, they insisted on helping crew the ship to the Golden Horn in exchange for immediate freedom. The leader of the slaves, from Ukraine, was called Lincolnella; she gave her word that they would assist in any way they could.

As she exchanged an imperial vessel for a pirate one, Theodora passed on the letter for the king to the captain.

"We are going back to Constantinople. I can't abandon the emperor."

The captain nodded in agreement.

"Besides, Trebizond doesn't look like my type of city anyway!"

Soon enough the winds were in support of her pirate ship, finally good weather. "An omen from the Virgin Mary, protector of Constantinople," she thought, looking up toward heaven.

Chapter 26

Genoese boat returns from Aegean

A day before the Fourth of May, it was time for a vessel to be dispatched and sent forth to the Aegean, in search of a relieving fleet.

I arranged a war council that included the emperor, Giustiniani, Notaras, Don Francisco de Toledo representing the Catalans, Venetian leaders and senior clergy.

The emperor was emotional.

"We are under siege in every direction, with at least 120 cannon balls pounding our walls day, and night."

Some of the Venetians, feeling the stress urged the emperor to leave the city. "If you leave and head to the Morea, you can rule what remains of the empire from Mystra. You can make an appeal to Europe for a crusade to be led by you and return to reclaim the city. That way Constantinople is spared, and we can return with a force. And vengeance."

Omitting to consider that Venice would therefore keep its trading empire, and the fact there was no guarantee that the republics would have the stomach for a war against the sultan at a later date.

Giustiniani shook his head. His blonde hair and blue eyes were filled with annoyance at the Venetians, dared not say anything until Constantine spoke.

"I cannot abandon Constantinople." With tears streaking down his cheeks, the well-built Greek-Serbian was feeling the strain of the campaign. "I shall not be leaving from my city. My mother, Helena, always taught me to stay strong in the face of any adversity." Turning to the Venetians, "can you dispatch a boat to the Aegean? The fastest you have, to see if a relieving fleet is sailing to help us."

With agreeable nods, he Venetians, acquiesced the request. Some volunteered to depart immediately. Within an hour, a dozen had been rounded up by the Venetian bailey and escorted to the harbour. With less than 40 boats remaining for the allies, it was hoped that the departure of one would not weaken the defences too much. The boat was quietly towed out, passing the temporarily unhatched chain on the Galata end; the vessel was sporting an Ottoman flag as it glided out at some point after midnight. The enemy did not pay any attention. However, inside the safety of the city, the emperor and Giustiniani paid careful attention. They prayed that the fleet was nearby, merely lost and waiting for an escort from these brave Venetian volunteers. A human form of *Venetian Point System,* or as some may name it, a VPS navigator.

Chapter 27

Tunnel Vision

The Venetian volunteers sped like lightening across the north end of the Aegean, passing Gallipoli, Imvros, Lemnos, Lesvos and reaching as far as Andros. At each port the assigned leader jumped into the port like a mad man and frantically asked the port captain for any sightings of the Venetian fleet, or any relieving fleet. Each port was the same. Not because they looked the same, rather it was because no one had heard anything. People were shocked about the situation in Constantinople and offered supplies and icons. With no time to spare, the Venetians would turn back and speed away to another destination. It was their version of a CONtiki tour. Within a fortnight, the crew had become bewildered and knew that no fleet would be arriving from the republics.

The crew were at the picturesque Mytilene harbour and decided to discuss the situation. Whether to take flight or return to Constantinople.

"We must abandon Constantinople and take comfort in a friendly port, we shan't return." Came one very loud voice amongst the volunteers upon debating whether or not they should return.

"The emperor entrusted us with this difficult task, and we must return to him, by the grace of God." Came a well-argued retort.

The Venetians debated what would be the best course of action as the boat lay for a temporary reprieve at the harbour.

As a group of eagles swooped overhead, a vote was taken. Democracy in the land of its birth was cruel to the dissenters and the vote revealed a willingness of the majority of crew to return to Constantinople. With no time to spare, the crew took advantage of the generosity provided by Poseidon of a flat sea and prevailing winds. They reached the Sea of Marmara just five days later. The Ottoman fleet were not to be deceived this time and in an awkward moment of "I can see you guys," the enemy came chasing. Yet again the fleet was called into action against Italian sailors. This time it was one boat against the Ottoman biremes. Baltoghlu was not around to be blamed if this attempt to capture a solitary vessel failed. This time, the result was rather different in many ways.

No battle was fought to underline how inferior the Ottoman navy was. Instead the volunteers easily manoeuvred and sped past the slower and poorly trained (by comparison) enemy fleet. The chain was opened, and the Venetians slid back in the Golden Horn. Far too easy for the crew.

"Why they gave up certain freedom for certain death, only their hearts and honour will truly know." This is all that I could muster in words, nudging my friend, the Basileus as I said it. "I wonder who else made bets with Grant that they would not return. All of the Genoans except Giustiniani took that bet."

The volunteers reached the emperor and recounted their mission. 'Mission unaccomplished,' is how it was viewed. The failure of any relieving fleet coming to aid Constantinople was distressing to everyone. The emperor embraced all of these exhausted sailors and ordered that each be given new dress pants, tunic and dalmatica as well as recently made Venetian boots as a sign of gratitude.

I always wondered if that fleet had shown itself, how quickly the siege would have been lifted. There is no doubt the Venetians would have destroyed the enemy fleet, and their cannons would have matched those of the Ottomans on the ground. Their supplies, their fighters and above all their presence would have saved us. Then again, I am just a chronicler, and I may be wrong. Little did we know that the fleet was just off the Greek coast and the fleet that the pope had ordered from Venice, was still under construction there. Ahhhhh. The frustration was immense. Just a small fleet is all we needed.

The emperor openly wept when the volunteers had departed. It was now just a matter of time.

Chapter 28

A good time to be a miner

Novo Brdo was a prosperous city in Serbia, one of the most important in the region. It was a hub for mines and miners including the predominantly German mining group who were now camped outside Constantinople. Or should I say underneath it.

The grand vizier had tasked them with taking the Greek technique of Trojan warfare and applying it to the siege. They would make it into the city at night to unlock the gates ala the ancient Greeks in Troy. Except rather than a wooden horse, they would employ mines as the secret weapon. Of course there was no Helen to fight over, in this story.

The sultan had wisely deduced that the defenders were not going to be toppled that easily thanks to the strength of the walls, as well as their resilience.

Starting, approximately, 150 metres from the walls, a series of tunnels were dug by a mixture of German and Ottoman sappers, on 15 May. No one in the city suspected the mining, for they were well hidden behind tents and other divisionary measures.

The miners dug down and then across using confined spaces and beams to hold up the tunnels. Not a good place to be if you were claustrophobic, or an orange obese.

⋆⋆

I was taking a walk along the ramparts with Grant and Giustiniani when I could sense some movement, some type of shaking. Grant quickly called for a bowl of water. Not because we had a thirsty dog. It was a good way to measure sudden ground movement.

Giustiniani ordered that bowls be placed all the way across our walls and to notify his favourite, and only, Scottish engineer if there was any sudden jerking or ripples. I was tempted to take a quick sip from the bowl as I had been somewhat dehydrated from a very warm day, placing the bowl by my feet. We watched for sudden jerks—no, not the Ottomans, I mean movements in the bowl. Sure enough there was. Grant knew instantly there was work being carried out directly beneath us, 70 metres below.

With the help of the Genoans and some of the Arab merchants, we dug a counter mine. Simultaneously, Grant offered the bet that we would dig the counter mine within a day, and we would nail these sappers.

As always, he was correct. We owed him buckets of water and goodwill. Grant surprised the sappers. We knew we had to be quiet to enjoy the element of surprise. Once Grant understood that their mine was meeting ours, we burst through and delivered a round of Greek fire followed by hand to hand combat. The poor sappers either died from the fright of seeing a ginger man and a mixed bag of Greeks and Genoans, or were easily cut to bits as fighting was not one of their skills. We collapsed the mine and celebrated above land. With Scotch.

We did not detect any further mines for five days. Grant suddenly located one as he had placed a bottle of alcohol, (we called it scotch, in his honour) on a wooden bench, which subsequently vibrated. The bottle then slid to the ground below. A waste of a good drink, to be honest. He worked out that their mine had passed under the foundations of the walls and into the city. This time the sappers were alert to us, withdrawing like stealth, collapsing the mine behind them, lest we converge on their camp.

From that moment on, a series of mines were detected. Each occasion a discovery was made, it became a stroll in the park. Their miners were tired by the time they reached the city, easy pickings for our fighters. We lost very few men. The enemy gave up about 200, perhaps more. Their fatigue and lack of military training was evident. I even felt sorry for them and began wishing that they would send some of their Janissaries to confront us. This rout of the enemy became the talk of Constantinople as people came to watch the entrances of the tunnels; who would come out and when? Others, like the Greeks or Venetians came as they wanted to join the action. By the time of the 25th of May, even members of the Varangian Guard and the Catalans had been in the mines with us. Citizens would come with icons, food, water and comfort. Yes, it does sound easy. Believe me, digging tunnels can be laborious and it has to be systematic, well organised and quiet.

This last tunnel was the one we almost missed as it ran directly under the walls at a right angle where cannon balls had been smashing the resistance. This tunnel was designed to be blown up by the enemy in an attempt to collapse the wall where the cannon balls had been targeting.

Grant had sensed something was occurring at around lunchtime, "call it a hunch." We managed to negate the attempt to blow the foundations, taking out the sappers. After patching up the mine, we managed to drag out two of the enemy miners. They had been beaten heavily by some of the Greeks. They were bloodied and bruised.

One of the Venetians had a grand idea to behead them after torturing them for information. I was appalled at this and the idea of throwing their heads over the wall. Of course, the Ottomans had also played that game starting with the beheading of the Venetian Captain Rizzo and some of his crew at Rumeli Hisar, the previous year; it was simply barbaric and cruel. I now completely understood why one side called the other dogs, usually spitting when they did that. Of course, if we also displayed a cruel side, the taunt of dogs would be levelled at us. There should be no dogs here, on either side. We are all humans.

This is what war and battles can do. Logic was not the prime focus for many. The mental strain for all those in the siege was there to be seen, driving occasional poor decision making. Could I blame them?

⋆⋆

We had succeeded in containing the mines. At the same time, the defenders also had to deal with mobile towers that were built and wheeled out to meet our walls. The sultan was always thinking. It is hard to believe he was a young man. Not content with going underground, he very nearly took us from the sky, as if he were part magician and part eagle with his stealth.

We maintained vigilance across the entire length of the walls. Our fleet kept an eye on theirs. Daily, Grant would be scouring the walls with Giustiniani to see what mines were being dug to snuff them out. It was taxing work, and they say the Muslim doesn't pay taxes, only the Christians do. Well it appears we certainly were paying! Dealing with all of that, our defences now had to deal with several wooden siege towers that now stood beside our exterior walls.

The speed of construction was phenomenal, built within a day. Archers had originally prevented us from countering, and we dared not come out to fight. Our numbers were down to about 7,100 and it is likely the attackers still had 90,000 fighters. We could not afford to lose more bodies.

Mehmed felt that if just two of the towers were tall enough above us, he could drop troops over the walls. If any of the mines worked, along with the constant cannon bombardment, he would have us.

"Commanders, let the men know that whoever can land on the other side and raise our banner, they will be rewarded like never before." Zaganos immediately thought of Hasan who dreamt of such a moment.

"My sultan we are in pole position, literally, and I can foresee a quick victory. I will provide the encouragement to the men," came the reply.

The sultan, pleased, nodded and stroked his beard in thought. He was already thinking ahead to the next phase, should this not succeed.

Despite all the strategic thinking and grand gestures, the enemy had overlooked one key element. A construct that relied heavily on wooden structures.

Giustiniani and the emperor did not even need to discuss the options. As one of those monster structures towered over our walls, out came the Greek Fire, bales of hay and archers. The structures stood no chance.

Giustiniani seized the moment and led some of his men outside the gates to take advantage of the smoke and confusion to strike down any of the retreating cowards. Cowards. For a few moments earlier they were happy to taunt the defenders as they felt they had the advantage.

"We will tear you down dogs. We will have our way with your women. Dogs. You will be punished." They grimaced.

The mini massacre outside the ditches demonstrated who actually was being punished. The Catalan leader dragged one man by the hair. He had been taunting the Catalan all day, who was now smiling. The sultan's soldier was begging in a language he could not comprehend.

“What are you saying? I only speak Catalan; However, I am sure you were calling me some sort of animal. This beast will now live up to your insult.” No one is quite sure what the Catalan did with the poor unfortunate being. He had a reputation for being tolerant to those who offered him respect and brutal to those who crossed him. Decades of mercenary adventures had not tempered the beast which lay deep inside him.

Chapter 29

Ottoman boats slip in

This was not the first time in the campaign that the sultan proved his genius. On 22 April, he pulled off one of the most incredible moments in siege warfare. The sultan was perhaps a younger version of the emperor. A thinker, swift leader, able to use his resources; takes advantage of whatever situation the universe provided.

Almost from the moment the Ottomans had arrived, the sultan had been toying with how to deal with the fleet in the Golden Horn. His own fleet had failed against the allies repeatedly and the chain was not going to be breached.

"If the Golden Horn is in accessible from the Marmara, then I will simply take my ships around by land," he explained to his closest confidants.

⋆⋆

"Emperor, emperor! Hurry, you need to see this."

It was Irene, she had been dispatched by Sphrantzes to find Constantine.

"Oh dear God, what now," he mumbled. It was 6 am, having fallen asleep at 2.30 am, a late finish from touring the defences. Throwing on imperial regalia and purple socks with his insignia, he jumped on his horse. His speedy horse was known as Bucephalus. He sped to the eastern perimeter where he met Sphrantzes.

"George, why would you wake me before 6.19?" He managed a slight dig at his secretary despite the circumstances. "I am a mere mortal and still need some sleep."

"Constantine, look at the far end of the horn."

Astonished, the emperor was baffled. "How in God's name did they manage to do that, how?

"They appear to have built roads with a group of Anatolian engineers and labourers. They had woodcutters lobbing trees for days. They used oxen, hundreds of men, ropes, and other material to hold and balance their ships. Using the logs, they rolled the ships on the logs and into the Horn. It is hard to believe; the ships appear to have balanced and made it into the water. As you can see, there must be seven in the water already and perhaps another 40 to roll out. These are their lightest and smallest vessels, though I assume all will be fitted with cannons."

Replying to Sphrantzes, without gazing away from the latest triumph from the sultan, "it will really stretch our defences now. It shall mean all sections of the walls will need to be vigilant with enough watchers. Our fleet will also need to be ready nonstop." He let out a loud sigh.

"Sphrantzes, call a meeting with Giustiniani, Notaras and the Venetian captains. We will need to act with stealth."

The secretary nodded as a group of eagles landed on the Ottoman fleet.

⋆ ⋆

The sultan knew that the Genoese were playing a double game. Many would sell products including oil for the cannons and other machinery by day and by night, many of the same people would come across the Horn to undertake a lookout shift with their fellow Christians. They also knew Giustiniani and were not about to let down one of their own.

The walls of Galata allowed the chain on the Golden Horn to connect with Constantinople. The sultan did not want to provoke Genoa or any of their colonies to come to the aid of Galata; preferring to allow them to play this potential deadly double game.

Notaras always felt that Galata were in an unenviable position, however, if they had just made the effort to join the defence, if, it is possible the Genoese colonies would have sent ships from the Black Sea and elsewhere. "How many of the citizens, of the republics, placed profit and greed over doing what was right," he would say to me. "The Ottomans will come for them, eventually, why not just combine our resources?"

⋆ ⋆

The sultan was sure that if his fleet made it into the Horn, Galata would remain neutral for the entirety of the campaign. It was a small walled city, though it contained several thousand fighters and had the resources to withstand a siege.

Therefore, it came as no surprise that the leaders of Galata had not informed the emperor that they suspected the movement of the Ottomans from the north on the Asiatic side, for days.

Giustiniani was not happy at all and dispatched a messenger to his fellow Genoans expressing his displeasure at the lack of 'vigilance.' He asked that some of the eyes of their scouts and tower guards should be tested. Perhaps, vision impairment had afflicted some of them.

The Venetians immediately blamed the Genoans, "this is a form of collusion with the enemy, quid pro quo from the sultan to the

Galata podesa." *The podesa is the equivalent of the Venetian bailey, in place to lead their people.* That was the reaction from the Venetians, as the ships were lowered one by one into the Horn at a time in the morning when most in the city were at church.

A small crew came aboard the first ship for a maiden Horn journey, accompanied by a group of musicians. They rowed close to the city and played to, literally, a captive audience. No one sought an encore!

Meanwhile, Zaganos was ensuring the land walls, at various points, were being hammered, adding to the sense of frustration for the defenders. People came out of the churches to the news that Constantinople was about to fall. Panic and despair set in for many. Others went back into the churches to pray.

For cardinal Isodore, he prayed harder and louder for the pope and the Venetians to send some relief, as promised.

Chapter 30

Counterattack Failure

My name is Giacomo Coco, I am 40 years old. A proud Venetian, I mastered the high and low seas. I arrived from Trebizond, a city I am fond of, in December. I showed the Turks at how good I am on water by easily outmanoeuvring their pathetic Rumeli Hisar fort which is designed to act as a check on ships passing through from the Black Sea.

On the water, I am better than most. My crew and I are slick, we are fast, coordinated and have a strong bond. We really are a premier team. Some people call us men or man united.

I was as angry as anyone when I saw what the sultan and Zaganos had conjured up. The Greeks provided begrudging admiration. I will admire them when they are in their graves. Big deal, they managed to use excess and slave labour to bring the ships over the peninsular. We do this in Venice all the time. In fact, it is like exercising in the gymnasium.

On the morning of the next day, a meeting was held at St Mary's Church. There were a dozen Venetian captains and the bailey of Venice, one Genoan who we all respect, the emperor and Sphrantzes. Outside it had been windy and the men had ridden against the wind to the palace.

The emperor had chosen to keep the meeting secret from the Genoans except Giustiniani. He wanted to keep a possible counterattack secret. The fact that lookouts from Galata had not 'seen' any movement troubled him. Was the governing pedosa playing a dangerous double game? The emperor did not have the time to ponder further, he needed a plan that would rid the Horn of this unsightly and most venomous of intruders.

He proposed to send a small flotilla at night to burn down the ships. The solution was an acceptable one and the Genoese are not to be informed. I never trusted them; it would be suicidal to tell them.

At the meeting, everyone took it in turns to have their say on how the attack would occur. A number of voices were in favour of leading a group of soldiers to take out the cannons protecting the fleet and then take on the enemy ships. Others had wanted an immediate full-frontal attack in daylight.

I had another option that was considered and voted on by the battle council.

"We attack late at night with a small group of ships and boats. We row as close to the enemy as possible before launching Greek fire, bails, bottled oil and anything else that explodes. Two of our best galleys shall follow to repel any counterattack. The enemy will be taken by surprise and considering the material of their vessels, we will be able to disable and destroy all of them."

The bailey said what many were thinking, "sounds like a shock and awe/oar plan!"

Outside the church, a man in a red shirt slowly swept the footpaths. It was good to see the church receive attention like that, though he should have been on the walls. He kept his head down and ears low. . . .

⋆⋆

This was the plan that was agreed to sans Genoese. I spent the next day preparing the logistics for the attack, supposedly in secrecy. Yet somehow, those pesky Genoans heard about the operation and demanded participation as if Athenian democracy had been restored in an imperial empire! My name is Coco, not Solon.

The bailey and the emperor relented. The Genoans did not want *to miss out* on the glory to the Venetians. There had already been several fisticuffs between us since the siege commenced. I really wanted to deck them now, and by deck, I am not referring to my ship.

This poorly thought out decision to allow them to participate, was further fraught with danger as we agreed to allow them four days to prepare their vessels. I mean, why did they require the four days? Cleaning, painting, waxing, a day off to pray, drills. Frustrating.

⋆⋆

It was 28 April; the moonlight and a slight breeze came across the Horn, most of the defenders had retired to their homes, replaced by non-fighters at the walls.

Around 400 men dashed out to their vessels.

I directed one of the three fustes. A fusta was a narrow, light and quick ship with which could be powered by sails or oars which holds two or three cannons. The fustes's mission being to destroy the enemy boats and were protected by two large Venetian galleys and a group of smaller boats and two transport ships.

"Something does not feel right." I turned to my deputy Dolfini. "It is too quiet for my liking." My deputy stared ahead, looking intently for any signs of movement.

Giustiniani, who was on a Genoese transport too was thinking how quiet it was. After all, dawn would be approaching, though this was just too calm. Behind him, a small flicker of light from a tower at Galata flickered.

I could order the attackers to return to the city, just a kilometre behind us, or I could power ahead of the armada. I chose the latter.

"Power ahead, do it quickly."

In Galata, a smallish light flickered. A man in a red shirt was spotted on the high tower, then abruptly departing with his head bowed back into the main piazza.

⋆⋆

In this way, Coco may have saved the armada by pushing his boat first. As the fusta sped ahead at light speed, a barrage of cannon fire rained down upon them. The fusta was no match for the volleys and sank without a trace, dooming all who were on board including Coco.

At once numerous ships and boats surrounded the allied ships and a gun battle took place until dawn broke. Each lost a boat, before both sides disengaged.

Some of the sailors from the second ship that sank swam as a pack to shore.... Where Zaganos was waiting for them.

"Do you want to live or die?" barked the commander.

"Go to hell you dog, Traitorous dog," came the reply of the captured Italian sailors.

"Very well, hell it is."

Zaganos turning to the sultan for approval, then turned to his deputy.

"Impale them."

By the afternoon, some 40 men had been impaled on the European side of the Horn in full view of the city. To add to the loss of an equal amount in the Horn just a few hours earlier.

⋆⋆

"Sphrantzes, we have about 260 prisoners inside Constantinople. On my orders you may have them executed immediately."

It was Notaras pulling his rank on me and responding at the atrocity that the whole city has witnessed.

Within an hour, numerous had been executed and allowed to dangle on the walls facing the impaled Italians.

"How is it we have a God, they have Allah, both are merciful, yet here we are killing people? I wonder how we can seriously justify this behaviour in the afterlife," I commented to Orhan who acknowledged my pain, before replying. "There should be no dogs here, yet all that I can see today are dogs. It is an unnecessary killing from both sides."

The failure to take out the fleet added to tensions between Venetians and Genoese. The unfortunate delay provided time for word to filter to Zaganos and the sultan, to prepare for the attack by Coco. Coco at the last moment was aware that they were betrayed and decided to sacrifice himself for the greater good of those behind him, saving a few in the process. Now, if only Venice and other powerful cities would sacrifice somewhat and come to the aid of our gallant defenders.

Chapter 31

A Scottish Tragedy

I have already explained to you who I am, Grant, your favourite (and only) Scotsman. A whirlwind romance in a city by the sea. Does that not count as a honeymoon? I have never been as happy, despite the bitterness of having to fight a ghastly enemy. There are 24 hours in the day. I sleep for six, I serve the emperor for 15 hours, I take bets for an hour—hey, we all need a side gig, and the final two hours are the best. Priceless hours. Irene accompanies me on some of the campaign tasks and acts as my partner when taking bets. Someone has to control the urge of 'gamblers' wanting to splurge by offering souvenirs taken from captives, shrapnel from the cannon blasts, material from failed attempts to breach the wall and 'IOUs.' Always happy to take a bet on what the Turks will screw up on a daily basis and how well our defences will hold. Maybe, it was my sense of humour that endeared me to all the races defending the walls. Maybe, it was the fact that gambling was never part of the vernacular here, hence being looked at with curiosity mixed with warmth

I enjoyed it immensely, as I bonded with defenders and spent ever more precious time with the love of my life. A short life as it was turning out.

Whenever we kissed, touched, talked or just shared a daily meal, my life felt precious. There were no flowers that I could give her. She did complain that I was being cheap by not holding a proper wedding party! That was when I decided to take her out to one of the ramparts where Prince Orhan was defending. His section was deemed the easiest to defend as it was high, well protected and was rarely being troubled by the enemy. We danced and we laughed, and I pointed out the invaders a good distance away, with their canon fire, well that was the *party*. All these guests and fireworks! "You are one lucky lass." I whispered into her ear.

Having dismantled my fourteenth mine and likely the last one that the enemy will attempt, we decided to celebrate with a romantic evening walk along the inner walls. This had become a routine; taking in the defensive line, talking to the soldiers, delivering any supplies from Sphrantzes and taking the odd bet! We had always been careful. We knew the risks associated with being near any wall. We all have a duty to contribute, even in down time. There were many stolen kisses on those walkarounds.

A blast hit the wall in front of us. It was from the monster cannon that Orban had built. Part of the tower in front of us crumbled. It felt like an earthquake. Fortunately, no one was hurt.

It was also our duty to help affect an immediate repair. A small group of us created a working bee. We all knew the drill to manage the repair. Stones, plaster and other material. The Greeks called for an icon and a priest to come and bless the work. We began reconstructing under my direction. I moved closer to the stone mason for a chat and to survey for additional damage along the perimeter.

BOOM. Another volley hit, this one not as strong as the previous shot. Most likely it was from one of the lesser cannon contraptions. How accurate it was. I can only imagine that the enemy think this constant bombardment will work, perhaps wear us down as it's not likely it will bring the walls of Theodosius down.

I looked around for my beautiful sweetheart. My eyes are good at scanning; comes with the mining territory, being able to see and grasp the surroundings quicker than most.

A large slab had come down, near where we stood. There was dust everywhere. The enemy could be heard celebrating, as they always do without understanding that minimal damage occurs to our spirit. Thankfully, none of the men were killed. Relief. Except, except, a solitary woman.... A petite body under a thick slab. I had to look away, suppressing a sob and a feeling of guilt and rage.

Chapter 32

Immortal Emperor, 28th May

There had been moments in the siege when losses for the sultan had been severe. On the twelfth day of the campaign, 18,000 had perished, which is the equivalent of approximately a third of the people in Constantinople. Shortly thereafter, the sultan had mulled over whether to retreat, in exchange for a massive indemnity. Aside from being nudged out of that thinking by Zaganos and a few others within his inner circle, or square (based on the outline of his tent), there was the small matter of paying the fee.

"What does he think we are, bankers?" Came the response from Notaras, who had already sanctioned his staff to periodically tour churches and other public buildings in search of gold or gold items that could be used to pay some of the foreigners.

Just over a month later, an ambassador was dispatched a few hundred metres to Constantinople. Unlike the brutal slayings of messengers before the siege began, Constantine received them with a courteous manner.

"We are here to allow the city a chance of life. We will allow

Figure 32.1: The last emperor of Byzantium. Image courtesy of *CC Graphics*.

you to leave the city and any person who fears the clemency of the Sultan, be assured that no harm will come to Constantinople or those who choose to remain."

The emperor frowned and allowed the smartly dressed, turban wearing speaker to continue. The Turban was used as a way for Muslims to be distinguished from non-Muslims.

"The sultan will recognise you as the ruler of the Morea and. . . "

"Let me halt you there, ambassador. If the sultan leaves now, we will gladly pay a larger tribute. Reluctantly, I will allow him to maintain the castles and lands he has taken from us in Thrace. Moreover, no harm will come to him from our empire. Your sultan, must understand, that I am unable to surrender Constantinople, to anyone, with the exception of God."

"Very well," came the acknowledged reply.

"One more thing ambassador. If the sultan wishes a one on one dual, this I am happy to accommodate. I am more than double his age; he should be energetic and robust enough to defeat this veteran."

The ambassador did not humour the emperor with a reply. He promptly turned and was escorted out of the city by a band of Greek fighters. The fighters were led by Commander Kantakouzenos, a descendant of misguided emperors and nobility from over a century before, whose civil wars and intrigue harmed the longevity of the city. The commander was trusted by the emperor, though took no chances, allocating him the safe post of the land walls facing the Golden Horn.

⋆⋆

"Forgive me. Forgive me."

The emperor had tears in his eyes.

"If I have ever wronged you, done harm by you, please accept my apology."

As his secretary, I was visibly shaken, knowing that this could be the last time I ever see my friend. Earlier, a message had come through via spies, likely from Hilal Pasha or the Serbs in camp, that a huge blitz would be expected. The gates of hell could be waiting for many transgressors, or the pearls of heaven for those simply following their civic duty.

"I am grateful to know each and every one of you."

The emperor moved from one to the other and kissed them on both cheeks. Many had tears running down their cheeks. This was not a sign of weakness; this was the sign of camaraderie and passion of people who felt closer, than at any other time of their lives.

"Grant, you have grown on me. A breath of fresh air and a stage for all of us to have a smile. A gateway to the Highlands. I want to meet your people one day, in this life or another. I take the loss of Irene personally, I am devastated for you and for me. I have felt that pain twice before. May she be remembered in eternity and until you shall meet again, Zwh se sas."

"Sphrantzes, what can I say about the most trustworthy and brilliant diplomat I have ever encountered." We both know what we had seen in our lifetime, across what remained of the empire. The fighting, diplomacy, the people and the attempt to manage what we had. Tough years." He reflected.

"Lukas, if only you were the chief minister of a far larger empire, your talents would have shone far greater. We are the richer for your unfailing duty to serve God and the empire."

"Giustiniani, words fail me.... And not because my Latin is letting me down today! I am emotional at the thought of what you gave up to come here with your troops. Genoa has never had a finer citizen."

"Senor Minotto, our Venetian bailey, you were always trying to make the last ounce of nomisma from me, yet when the time came, I became full of admiration that you put your trust in friendship rather than commercial considerations. You have led the Venetians admirably."

"Dr Barbaro, you have brought honour to medicine. Sphrantzes tells me you are chronicling the story of the defence. I wish to read your account one day. Here, or in heaven."

"Cardinal, you have a thankless task in trying to unite us all in the house of God. I appreciate what you have brought to us and I hope to hear more of your adventures and misadventures in Europe, when this is over."

"Catalan, I would follow you into any battle my friend. Just as I am looking forward to seeing what the Highlands are, I want to see where you were born. I am no fan of this bull fighting you tell me exists in Iberia, perhaps, I will try it once without maiming the animal."

It went on, as everyone in the large dining hall that served as campaign headquarters was embraced with warm words. Few people spoke, as grown warriors were now displaying a vulnerability that had been absent against the enemy.

The emperor then embraced all workers at the palace. He never had to hide feelings of gratitude to those who served him, diligently.

"Now let us follow the cardinal to the sermon, where the name of the pope and my own, will be commemorated. Then I want you all to go home to your families and return past the midnight hour to your posts.

Later that evening, the emperor gave the following speech, part of which I have recorded here:

"Most noble leader, illustrious tribunes, generals, most courageous fellow soldiers and all loyal honest citizens! You know very well that the hour has come: the enemy of our faith wishes to oppress us even more closely by sea and land with all his engines and skill to attack us with the entire strength of this siege force, as a snake about to spew its venom; he is in a hurry to devour us, like a savage lion. For this reason I am imploring you to fight like men with brave souls, as you have done from the beginning up to this day, against the enemy of our faith. I hand over to you my glorious, famous, respected, noble city, the shining Queen of cities, our homeland. You know well, my brothers, that we have four obligations in common, which force us to prefer death over survival: first our faith and piety; second our homeland; third, the emperor anointed by the Lord and fourth; our relatives and friends.

"Well, my brothers, if we must fight for one of these obligations, we will be even more liable under the command strength of all four; as you can clearly understand. If God grants victory to the impious because of my own sins, we will endanger our lives for our holy faith, which Christ gave us with his own blood. This is most important of all. Even if one gains the entire world but loses his soul in the process, what will it benefit? Second, we will be deprived of such famous homeland and of our liberty. Third, our empire, renowned in the past but presently humbled, low and exhausted, will be ruled by a tyrant and an impious man. Fourth, we will be separated from our dearest children, wives and relatives.

"This wretch of a sultan has besieged our city up, with all his engines and strength; he has relaxed the blockade neither by day nor night, but, by the grace of Christ, our Lord, who sees all things, the enemy has often been repelled, up to now, from our walls with shame and dishonour. Yet now too, my brothers, feel no cowardice, even if small parts of our fortifications have collapsed from the explosions and engine missiles, as you can see, we made all possible, necessary repairs. We are placing all hope in the irresistible glory of God. Some have faith in armament, others in cavalry, might and numbers but we believe in the name of our Lord, our God and Saviour, and second, in our arms and strength granted to us by divine power.

"I know the countless hordes of the impious will advance against us, according to their custom, violently, confidently and with great courage and force in order to overwhelm and wear out our few defenders with hardship. They attempt to frighten us with loud yells and innumerable battle cries. You are all familiar with their chattering and I need say no more about it. For a long time they will continue so and will also release over us countless rocks, all sorts of arrows and missiles, like the sand of the sea. I hope that such things will not harm us; I see, greatly rejoice, and nourish with hopes in my mind that even if we are few, you are all experienced and seasoned warriors—courageous, brave, and well prepared. Protect your heads with shields in combat and battle. Keep your right hand, armed with the sword, extended in front of you at all times. Your helmets, breastplates and suits of armour are fully sufficient together with your other weapons and will prove very effective in battle. Our enemies have no and use no such weapons. You are protected inside the walls, while they will advance without cover and with toil.

"For these reasons, my fellow soldiers, prepare yourselves, be firm, and remain valiant, for the pity of God. Take your example from the few elephants of the Carthaginians and how they dispersed the numerous cavalry of the Romans with their noise and appearance. If one dumb beast put another to flight, we, the masters of horses and animals, can surely even do better against our advancing enemies, since they are dumb animals, worse even than pigs. Present your shield, swords, arrows, and spears to them, imagining that you are a hunting party after wild boars, so that the impious may learn that they are dealing not with dumb animals but with their lords and masters, the descendants of the Greeks and the Romans."

"Now he wants to enslave her and throw the yoke upon the Mistress of Citie, our holy churches, where the Holy Trinity was worshipped, where the Holy Ghost was glorified in hymns, where angels were heard praising in chant the deity of and the incarnation of God's word. He wants to turn into shrines of his blasphemy, shrines of the mad and false Prophet, Mohammed, as well as into stables for his horses and camels.

"Consider then ... how the commemoration of our death, our memory, fame and freedom can be rendered eternal."[1]

Many of the intended recipients wept. It was an emotional speech from a leader who loved his subjects as if all were related to him. This was no show, it was raw emotion.

[1]Part of the speech given by the emperor on 28 May 1453, recorded by Sphrantzes.

Chapter 33

Can't win with the sword, pray instead

Sometimes, you can see the eagles gently gliding in the skies above the church. Other times you can see a Holy light emanating from the highest dome, as if the saint and the Virgin Mary were in unison, seeking out the people, believers.

The evening of 28th May, Hagia Sofia was once again packed with worshippers. Many had stayed away from the magnificent church, ever since the 'union' with the Vatican was proclaimed. On this night, no one seemingly cared as the emperor, the cardinal, and hundreds of faithful were gathered inside and thousands more outside.

What had made this church special to the Greeks and indeed to many others? It was an architectural delight and builders' triumph, arguably an equal of ancient constructs known to the Athenians, Corinthians, Syracusan, Makedoni, Thebans, Romans, Persians, Carthaginians and Egyptians.

Originally, an East Roman cathedral sat here after the reign of Constantine I, and was called the 'Great Church' as it was by far one of the biggest religious places in the world. Sadly, the church lasted a mere few decades before crazy citizens in the city, destroyed this place of worship.

Over a century later, Justinian commissioned Isidore of Miletus and Anthemius of Tralles to design a new, larger church that would be known the world over. The empire was flushed with funds; Constantinople was the richest and most advanced city in the world. The nomisma currency was the world standard in currency, until the Latin Crusaders arrived 700 years later.

When the papal bull was placed at the alter at Hagia Sofia in 1054, the church essentially became the Greek Orthodox Church. Greek was the language of liturgy anyway and the saints were usually Greek!

The Crusaders, temporarily occupying the city, converted the church to the ways of the Vatican; though the pope was unimpressed with their treachery. Fortunately, Michael Palaiologos regained Constantinople and eliminated from our church and city, the scum who had plagued the empire. I worry that the sultan will turn this into a mosque by adding minarets, or a museum. As the church is built with a combination of sand, brick, and minute ceramic elements, it would be hard for us, or them, to destroy what belongs to heaven and the Virgin Mary. You will also note the impressive frescoes across the walls and ceiling for the benefit of the faithful. The frescoes are painted to last. The iconographers probably provided a money back guarantee that it would last. And I believe them. *Six centuries from now, they will still be visible, unless they are painstakingly scrubbed off.*

This masterpiece appears to have been named after the martyr Sofia, yet in actuality it is *Wisdom of God, the Logos, which is the second person of the Trinity*, celebrated on 25th December. Ναός της Αγίας του Θεού Σοφίας, Naos tēs Hagias tou Theou Sophias.

The night before, as I seem to have become dazzled and distracted by the feeling of divinity, was a night when both the emperor and the Pope were commemorated in prayer at the church. A procession was held taking many large icons along the walls to highlight the faith and repudiation of what lay outside. Chanting. Beautiful symphonies of voices in song and prayer were heard. Candles were lit and the icons paraded. At the head of the procession was a large icon of the Virgin Mary. As the priests held the icon, the icon inexplicably fell from the frames holding the icon. People stopped singing, shocked. For we are a superstitious lot. Why did it have to fall?

"We are doomed, this cannot be a good omen," a few of the worshippers mumbled.

Just then, a light, a glow, a cloud, a whiteness, could be seen atop of the church. It disappeared into the evening skyline.

Across from the walls, Muslims inside the Ottoman camp prayed. Two days earlier, the devout had remembered the anniversary of the appearance of the first verses of the Quran. Today, they had been given a day off, having spent the previous day making intricate preparations for one final attack in what some called, Jihad. They too could see the bright light evaporate above.

⋆ ⋆

As a 12-year-old, Mehmed asked his tutors, "tell me about the ancient Greeks! Tell me about the ancient Persians!" This was less than a decade earlier. Mehmed studied the Quran. He studied his potential adversaries too. He asked questions just like a young Alexander had of Aristotle. Mehmed had a thirst for knowledge and a want for information on how to defeat these descendants of the ancient Greeks. The sultan had prepared most of his young life for the capture of Constantinople. He could speak all the important languages that were spoken in the city, and just like some of the Greeks and Venetians, he had a flair for reading and writing poetry.

The apple in his eye was close enough. As he allowed his troops a complete day of rest for what lay ahead, Mehmed, wore his large cylinder style turban, also known as a *mücevveze,* along with his favoured gold and silver plated and weaved robe and kaftan, most likely created by the special palace court designers, the *hassa nakkaşları*. With his sword on his belt, he looked every inch imperial and a potential new Caesar of the city he was desperately chasing. The sultan was sat with his commanders and viziers. Then they prayed for what must surely be an Ottoman victory.

Outside, the camp was full of life and colour. A contrast to the sombre mood a few hundred metres away, across ditches and walls that had been pummelled, almost ceaselessly for weeks.

⋆ ⋆

Further afield, on the sea, the mood was one of anxiety. Anxious to get back to the city by a pirate boat commandeered by an unusual 'seaman.'

Theodora urged the sailors on. She had not changed her white dress once since the ship had turned around from the coast of the Pontus.

"Hurry, hurry!" She kept urging the crew, and herself as she helped with whatever tasks were needed on the starboard or below the deck. There was no time to lose. One boat could make a difference.

The dreaded Rumeli Hisar, was approaching the horizon. Perhaps a day's sailing away. For the second time in a short period, the crew would try to outrun the infamous throat cutter which had sunk Rizzo.

Theodora scanned the skies for a glimpse of the Hagia Sophia. There was something else in the sky, she thought.

⋆ ⋆

When a chronicler compiles a story for any battle, they can do no worse than reference 29 May, for this was truly a decider in every respect, with two hard nosed and tough leaders on either side of the walls.

The Ottoman camp had remained festive. Zaganos and the sultan planned to attack the entire breadth of the wall. Those not immediately facing St Romanus Gate, were essentially dealing with walls that remained strong with minimal repairs.

Romanus had been breached by the massive cannon balls on nine occasions. The defenders had used every bit of smarts to repair the holes, using barrels, wax, debris, steel. Anything they could find to affect an instant repair and the threat of more cannon balls.

Grant had a question to his wife early in the campaign, "why would you people name a gate after an emperor who lost a battle to the Seljuks in Manzikert, thus paving the way for this rubbish situation?" It was an interesting question and one that she never answered.

Grant was on the outer wall. He was offered a key to the gate, but chose not to accept, as he wasn't sure of the state of his mind. He did wonder how sturdy the defence would be today. Along a stretch of some 400 metres as well as in the inner walls behind him, Grant estimated that there were close to 2000 troops. Giustiniani's talented forces, Cretans, Imperial forces, Varangians, some of the Venetians and what remained of the empire's nobility.

"All two of them," Grant mumbled to himself, daring not to think of his lost Irene.

Behind them was a reserve force of 300 soldiers. The reserve force had been double that size at the start of the siege, now this depleted group was on the ready to fill any section that could struggle against whatever came over those walls.

The emperor made the point that if Sparta could use 300 men, "then we could too."

"Did they not lose to the superior numbers of Persia?" It was Toledo offering a sobering history lesson.

A well-read Venetian, possibly Dr Barbaro, offered, "and we have many *Efialtes* (traitors) amongst the Genoans." Many of the Venetians were convinced that Galata housed many traitors.

⋆⋆

Mehmed took one last look at his Quran as he strolled confidently outside his tent. It could not have been easy to command men double and triple his age. Yet he managed to make his mark. If he lost the siege, these same 'elders' could turn on him. Many of the Janissaries were not completely won over, and Hilal missed his father Murad, whom he loyally served without question.

It was 1.30 am and with a nod from Zaganos, trumpets blared to herald the start of the next and possibly final phase of the campaign.

Chapter 34

Decider

The Ottoman officers called on the rag tag of expendable men to head for the walls first. Or rather head to a slaughter. They had little love for this group. They were depending on looting as their main inspiration to climb those walls, were lightly armed. They were truly a composite group of men.

Barbaro, the doctor on duty at Romanus, made a point to note for the compilation of his own chronicles. "Muslims, Barbarians, Germans, other Christians. What a strange group with a mixture of bows, scimitars, spears and many greedy eyes."

For the sultan, these may have been a rag tag bunch, but they were there to sap the energy of the defenders. Before breaking for their attack positions a few hours earlier, Zaganos had instructed these men to be ready to charge at a decent pace, when the attack is ordered. The ditches in front of them had, by now, been filled by the weeks of fighting and were easy to cross over. Some of the irregulars prepared to fire their arrows, while others brought wooden ladders.

"How do they not realise that wooden ladders will be burnt if we choose that course of action?" It was the Catalan leader voicing his approval of their stupidity to his friend the emperor.

The emperor simply shook his head and shrugged. “That is why they are fighting us, rather than standing tall on our side of these walls. Surely, they are missing brains and hearts.”

⋆ ⋆

The emperor now stepped forward. With his height, charisma, royal outfit and sword in his hand, he looked every inch imperial and ready to lead.

He had spent the last hour riding to key points on the wall to urge the defenders on.

“Men, women, citizens, friends. This is our last stand. Tonight, we will rise one more time and defeat the infidel. They call us dogs, yet we are not the ones running on four legs to steal a city that does not belong to them. We have come this far. Together, for we are all in this together, we will fight one more time. I will see you again for a celebration. May God be with you.”

The defenders all cheered. Some broke out into church hymns and chanting.

And now, at 1.40 am, the emperor addressed Romanus Gate, reminding all and sundry the honour they would now bring to themselves, “for no defenders in the history of warfare have stood as firm, tenacious and proud as you have. We have withstood them for 52 days. Now we can add a further day.”

Giustiniani waited until the emperor had finished his rousing speech and the cheering had slowed. Surveying the ladders and the resources he had, he simply demanded that the ladders be pushed back. The poorly thought out attack was seeing ladders failing. The enemy was being thrown onto the piles of debris over the ditches, in front of the outer wall.

Some of the more ingenuous attackers were able to use ropes to affix ladders. They were being shielded by a fierce volley of arrows emanating from the rear. This time, the second group of irregulars seemed to be making an impact.

Across the way, the sultan looked on, waiting for the next move from Giustiniani.

The Genoan simply called for Greek fire and oil to be spread across the wall. One by one, the ladders with ropes were burnt to ash.

More waves came to the wall. Cannons also blasted overhead. The defenders were not wavering.

"We have lost a small chunk of men, Constantine. I am calling in the reserve 300 to join us in the next hour as I can see more losses coming." It was the Genoan making the call.

The emperor nodded and took up his position to the left of Romanus. It was not unusual to see the emperor discuss instructions, encourage people or talk tactics with the Genoan. Those around him could be seen ducking and weaving stray arrows. The emperor had no such compunction; he felt that only Achilles could be struck from a stray arrow, and Achilles he was not. The beard and the difference in costume being some of the distinguishers.

Irregulars kept at it for two hours. Occasionally, some made it to the top of the wall where they were met by skilled fighters. Dead bodies of the enemy suddenly became the biggest impediment as their losses piled up.

The emperor ordered nonfighting citizens such as monks and nuns to dump the bodies back over the walls. It was a contrasting image, people of God disposing bodies while behind them, the occasional attacker who had made it over the wall was being brought down by swords, meeting a violent and unholy fate. At one point, a monk had to duck as a crazy attacker attempted to chop off his head as a souvenir for visiting the city. Fortunately, the emperor was a few metres away, and with a spear he had just picked up and threw it accurately before the attacker could try again.

Many irregulars had become irritated at the way the attack

was playing out and tried to return to camp. Commanders had anticipated the move and deployed elite soldiers with whips and swords to force them back to their near or certain death.

In this way, a sea of bodies would tell the story of thousands of deaths. This would be a perfect end for the campaign for the defenders, if only the sultan could take a hint and call it off.

Instead, he kept urging the fleet in the Horn to continue bombarding the walls as a demonstration of power, while preparing for the second phase attack at Romanus.

At some stage, after 3.30 am, the second assault was called upon. Cannon balls blasting as the second phase troops were being inspired by the sultan.

"For the glory of your Anatolian lands. For the glory of your sultan. You have history calling. These infidel are ready to be defeated. Go my good men, my friends, and take us to the promised Constantinople." Zaganos yelled.

The second wave consisted of better trained soldiers with stronger armour, significant military experience and a love for their sultan, rather merely looting. They marched in military precision, disciplined and with the learnings of the failed first attack as a guide. They also possessed more courage against a tired defence.

"Why don't you send back the other lot?" It was Grant lamenting how this was not a fair fight. Fresh fighters against exhausted spirits.

Unusual for this time of night, a number of eagles flew past the inner walls.

⋆ ⋆

Giustiniani, was just like the emperor. He understood how to lead and motivate from the frontline. There was no amount of convincing these two warriors, they would not budge from their positions.

Mehmed knew that if you cut off the head of the lion, it may deter the rest of the beasts and he had instructed the commanders at the earlier pre-war briefing to try hard to scale the point where emperor and the Genoan would meet every few minutes.

⋆⋆

The Anatolian soldiers with shields and determination were ironically not shielded well enough. A flood of arrows, rocks and small cannon balls smashed most of the front line. A monk expertly threw his cross, which smashed one soldier on the head.

The sultan was certainly someone with genius and smarts. Wise enough to avoid the frontline, he was shouting enthusiastically for his men to feel inspired. From afar.

Grant, yet again, leant next to the person and asked, "why doesn't he show the bravery of the emperor and lead the charging forces? I know he isn't that slim but surely he can canter slowly behind the front row of soldiers; or should I say, frontline corpses." He grinned in the darkness, proud at his sense of humour.

The Anatolian regiments pushed on. Some reaching the walls before meeting their makers, shortly after. Others used climbing equipment and ladders to generate an impression, before they too met their maker.

As the defenders had gained the edge, the Anatolian troops retreated to regroup. This temporary pause was fortuitous, for the gun of Orban, who had long since met his maker, delivered a form of redemption. A large ball smashed a hole; an invitation for the Anatolians to return with a sense of vengeance and purpose, as smoke, darkness of the evening and the yelling created a vertigo moment for the defenders. The attackers came thick and fast.

"Giustiniani, we need the hole patched," came frantic shouting.

"Giustiniani we need to retreat," came a voice from the Latins.

He knew exactly what was required to respond.

"Shortly, a few of their men will come through that hole. There is no need to panic. Carrying their shields, swords and body armour will tire them. Allow them to pour into the gap between the inner and outer wall. Francisco, take 20 of your finest Catalonians and stand with your backs to the inner wall. They will come at you. My troops, I need you to spread across the outer wall. When they come through the courtyard, as it is narrow, jump down and encircle them."

Continuing, "Greeks, I want a dozen of you on either side of the breach, at a distance. Let their first men pass. Then fire down every missile you can. Citizens, you have the toughest task. With the help of God, try to patch up that stupid hole. Nobody likes a hole like that. It looks unbecoming on such a beautiful wall."

The orders were obeyed with expediency. The Anatolians, incredulous at their success had a *what now*? moment and simply poured into the gap between inner and outer. 200 of them to be precise. Ready to take on the Catalans and the Genoans. Rushing toward them in a *rope a dope* Ali/Foreman moment, Toledo did not budge. The leader of the charging contingent did not understand why, until it was too late. Venetians, Genoans, Greeks and the Varangian Guards quickly encircled all of the invaders. One by one in quick succession, they were slashed and smashed. Not a soul survived. The emperor cheered from above and returned to martialling the wall.

⋆⋆

Elsewhere, Halil had tried another invasion from the Marmara, which was equally unsuccessful, though, Mehmed had expected that and certainly had lost faith in Halil to push as hard as possible. "I will deal with him when the time comes," he had confided in Zaganos.

In the Horn, the bombardment from the ships continued, though they were similarly unable to make a breach. This area proved a real humiliation, as it was defended by a mixture of monks, Greeks and Turks, men and some women. The Horn had proven to be a friend as the conditions in the water had been far from steady for what would normally be a good seafaring time of the year.

At the Blachernae Palace section, the Bocchiardi Brothers were as defiant as ever. Certainly Paolo, Troilo and Antonio, all the o's were not the type to take a backward step, and they were joined by Geronimo and Leonardo di Langasco, also brothers, and a few more of their Genoan friends. Between cursing the attackers and making fun of them, all the brothers seemingly enjoyed siege warfare. There was nothing that could shake these Venetians who fought under the flag of St Mark. The emperor joined in, with a quip, the previous evening with, "if I notice just a scratch on my palace behind you, I will hold you to account and withdraw you from further siege duties." The brothers laughed; it is claimed that the laughter may have caused one of the brothers to break a rib!

A frustrated sultan was now at his wit's end as runners kept delivering messages that no attack had succeeded at any of the points around the walls. One of his runners had the guile to report that the Bocchiardi brothers had even made a counterattack. Coming out of a locked gate, savaging dozens of the sultan's troops.

The poor showing of the Anatolians against the brave defenders ensured that thousands more had fallen, to add to the irregulars' list of fatalities. If points were given for body count, it is clear who the victor would be.

Four hours of fighting had come to this. He turned 180 degrees to see the Janissaries, lancers, personal bodyguards and the last of his elite forces. Thousands were ready to attack the weakest part of the wall. All told, there were now less than 7,000 exhausted soldiers spread across the entire length of the city. This number was topped up with monks, nuns, foreigners and citizens. Church bells rang as many citizens were reciting prayers at some of the churches.

⋆⋆

Mehmed gave the order. There was no time for he did not wish his enemy to recoup any energy with a respite. This was his last throw of the dice. His elite forces and Janissaries would significantly outnumber the defenders at Romanus. They were good odds for someone like Grant, should he have wished to create a bet spread.

Grant, this time, was focussed on one element. To avenge his wife's death by chopping down as many of the bastard enemy as he could. His eyes were wide eyed, and his heart was racing. Just like most of the defenders. At some moments, he was salivating and at other moments he was red with anger. "Come on you damn enemy, is that the best you have?" he roared.

⋆⋆

The elites were led by a range of disciplined heavy infantry, with Mehmed leading the way as far as the ditch in front of Romanus. Would the name of a disgraced emperor from a bygone era have yet another negative impact on the empire, or will there be redemption?

Mehmed ordered for a constant battery of archers, cannon, spears and any other projectile to land over the wall, taking out as many defenders as possible in the process. Under this cover, the elites made their dash. Many succeeded in attaching ladders, others used barrels that were hanging on the walls from the previous Greek fire torrents. The defenders tried to shower these attackers with rocks, javelins and dead bodies. The first *wave* was supressed. The second followed. The defenders would have preferred waves in the ocean to waves of potential death. Eventually, a good number made it on to the rampart with fierce and ferocious fighting taking place. Again, the defenders could claim the victory, only this time, a few of the defenders were also part of the casualties.

Both Giustiniani and the emperor repulsed attackers, with the nobility joining Constantine to eliminate a good number. Lifelong training and vigilance had steeled these fighters for such encounters.

The emperor was always in his element when he could use his sword.

The cardinal looked on proudly, knowing that victory was here and soon the Pope would send reinforcements to the city. Along with the reunification of the churches, he felt his work for God had been complete.

⋆⋆

"There is always a moment for a laugh and high confidence. There are moments like these when focus and conservative instincts should take place," Notaras noted to me, from a few hundred metres from the Blachernae Palace as he observed and responded to the carelessness of the brothers and their men. One of them, tasked with locking the gate behind them when returning from a daring attack, had failed to lock the gate behind them. Perhaps a moment of fatigue? Stupidity? It mattered not as a band of Ottomans snuck in. They quickly tore down the flags of the empire and the standard of St Mark and replaced them with the sultan's which gave the attackers outside a glimmer of hope.

Notaras sent some of his troops to help the brothers and their men; having been surprised, they were struggling to hold these determined intruders from inching further. The intruders were surrounded by the relief force, however, the loss of fighters was significant as was the morale boost to the outside invaders.

⋆⋆

Back at the Romanus Gate, the elites of the sultan had been defeated. Just a few more were willing to chance their luck against the crazy defenders.

Mehmed was preparing to decide. The moment of retreat was running through his head. Tens of thousands of soldiers had perished in the campaign with almost half on this day alone.

An Ottoman archer of merit, who would have been a noble entry to the ancient Greek Games, was able to take a shot. A shot that he had been wanting to undertake for the last hour. "Take out the leader of the lions and you have an advantage, if not a decisive one," he thought.

He could see the tall and muscled beared target, leading the troops. The archer could see how they listened, a man of honour and charisma. With one eye closed and the other focussed, he shot the arrow.

It missed. The eagle above him proved to be a distraction.

The sultan looked around, having now listened to more news from his runners. The stars were fading. The sun was being readied from a restless evening of sleep.

The archer took aim one last time. It flew through the air on an upward trajectory. It may have skimmed the tip of the wall and somehow it landed. The landing was through a gap in the armour of the Genoan. Who shot the arrow? I will never be sure.

⋆ ⋆

A buzz of drama and excitement ensued. Giustiniani took a step forward and collapsed. Immediately, he was rushed by some of his men. Barbaro was called to help the fallen hero.

"Can you take me to my ship for treatment? I do not wish to be treated up here as a distraction and if the enemy breach the line again. . . ."

Barbaro declined. "I think it wise you remain here." The Genoans therefore called for another medical practitioner, someone not aligned with Venice who could meet Giustiniani at his boat in the boom of the Horn.

The emperor was informed and told that the Genoan will be taken to his ship.

The emperor, without hesitation rushed to see the Genoan, who was bleeding and bruised at the point of penetration.

"How are you feeling? Status?"

Starting to feel the injury through the shock, the Genoan replied, "I need to get proper treatment. The medicine and tools we need are on my ship. The soldiers will hold the line."

The emperor was too experienced and seasoned enough to understand that a retreat would give the attackers hope.

The Janissaries were scouring the wall searching for any visual of the fallen Genoan. The sultan too was now informed of the situation.

"Commander, friend, please stay at your post. I beg of you with all my life, do not abandon us, not now." Came an impassioned plea from the emperor. "You are not a coward; you need to stay with us."

"I will return, you have my word. I just need to get the treatment."

A horrified emperor reluctantly allowed his struggling body to be stretchered away.

Despite the advantage held by the defenders, dozens of his troops followed their leader, like a puppy following their master. Except this was not a moment to play fetch. Victory was just there, and Giustiniani was there too. Then gone. This mini panic was soon exacerbated by more of his troops who thought their leader was fleeing the city, rather than realising the seriousness of the injury meant treatment on his boat

Dissent broke out between some of the Greeks and the Genoan's troops. In this ill-advised moment for debate, he ordered yet another 'final' surge.

"Allah Akbar" could be heard repeatedly, deafening.

The emperor rallied the Greeks and any of the remaining Genoans. An already tired and steadily depleted section on the ramparts would now need to find a strength that bellied their numbers. Outside, all available troops of every class made their way forward. This time, the Greek Fire was limited owing to lack of numbers and chemical ingredients.

Hasan Ulubatlı, a formidable member of the cavalry managed to climb the wall with a group of 30. He was just a few years older than his sultan. He had a sword, shield and the banner of the Sultan. He was promised *immortality* should he become the first person who could fly the flag of his empire. Clearly, the earlier achievement at the Blachernae palace walls had been forgotten by the enemy as Mehmed cheered and urged on Hasan from a distance. “Plant our banner, be the first,” could be heard.

The Greeks fought the invading group who proved no match for the ever-alert defenders. Hasan, however, held on to the banner, inspiring the thousands who were now throwing themselves into battle one last time, below. Hasan had shown you could make it across the wall and hold on.

Archers from the cardinal were using his broad body as target practise with a total of 27 arrows penetrating the body. Lastly, it appeared to be the gingered Grant, who had helped mop up the fighters, managed to plunge his sword into the banner holder. Finally collapsing, which seemingly coincided with the collapse of the defence on the outer wall; for suddenly more and more invaders starting pouring over the outer wall and some through it.

The overwhelming numbers of fighters meant that the defenders had to retreat. Now the numbers were a hundred to one.

⋆⋆

An almost tsunami of attackers was an impossibility to defend. Conjuring up the spirit of the heroes of Greece and Rome, they first tried to beat off the attack with significant losses. Then, they too looked for an exit. Some of the defenders managed to take the same gate of exit that Giustiniani used.

The emperor had one last card to play.

A reasoning with God. He prayed that if ever the Venetian fleet would appear, "then let it be now."

He called the remaining archers to face the onslaught.

"Grant, hide these please and you are free to flee like my coward friend." The emperor had taken off all his imperial regalia.

Grant nodded with his eyes popping out, filled with adrenaline. "Eh, but on the condition I die fighting at your side. I am not going anywhere, but I am taking these brutes with me to oblivion."

The emperor could not believe the courage of the Scotsman, who quickly scampered off to fulfil his task of hiding the imperial clothes.

The nobility stepped in front of the emperor as well as the common people. It was their moment, to truly earn their birthright. Up stepped Toledo and the emperor to join the nobility. Toledo himself was a member of the Spanish nobility, oddly having volunteered to make his way to defend a fellow Christian noble, he was accepted by the Catalonians to lead them despite not being a Catalan; some would say owing to his dashing, finely cut black outfits which presented him as a true noble.

A ferocious battle ensued. Arrows still flying despite a number of them being slain by Janissaries. One by one, the nobles were cut down.

Toledo and Constantine, sticking to a narrow confine, were able to hold off the villains. To their side, the Greeks held off any more attackers. Blood, bodies, yelling, screaming and the clanking of steel could be heard.

One side barking at the other.

An eagle swooped down just as one would be attacker tried to fell the emperor, distracting the assailant. Lucky.

A spear managed to hit the emperor. He simply pulled it out. boomeranging it back, killing a stunned Janissary.

The hand to hand fighting continuing for a good few minutes. The weight of numbers now became the challenge rather than the skill and standard of fighters. The Catalan trained in the art of grappling and bull fighting was now in a position to throw adversaries over the wall.

It was just a matter of time.

The Catalan and his companions were down on numbers and now detached from the emperor. The Janissaries had succeeded in removing all archers and had their own in reply. Archers focussed on the Catalonian contingent. Just like Leonidas, their last stand ended in a hail of arrows. *Glory in death* rang out in a chorus as these brave souls met their fate.

The emperor who was now surrounded, let out a yell for his friend. An enemy combatant managed to insert a knife in the lower back of the emperor. The soldier was unaware that it was the emperor he had injured. The emperor was struggling to lift his sword, having abandoned his shield. A soldier lunged forward to finish off the wounded Constantine. Here the typical courage of a real soldier can be evidenced; Grant dived forward, taking a fatal blow. With that reprieve, Constantine killed the attacker and slumped to his knees.

He stood up as a flock of eagles flew through the madness, creating a temporary distraction.

The Greeks and the remaining soldiers were all seemingly taken down by the sheer force of the numbers. A staggering Constantine tried. He tried. Blood seeping out of a number of injuries and cuts from sharp blades. Constantine was still trying to swing his sword, which now weighed heavily.

The sun was up, a blinding distraction. The attackers knew it was over, and instead turned to enter the city.

The sultan was proclaiming, “the city is taken, go forth and secure it." Just like a large statue in the city depicting Justinian pointing to Asia, the ruler from an Asian empire was now pointing to Constantinople. In victory.

Chapter 35

Cretans refuse to surrender

Across Constantinople, news travelled quickly; Constantinople had been taken and the barbarians were in the city. Nonfighting citizens rushed to their homes, or to churches.

Foreign fighters could see no way of retaliating and began heading in mass to the harbour. A sickly Giustiniani, now on his deathbed, was advised. Tears came to him. In a weakened voice, "rally up our survivors and set sail for Chios. They will go after loot initially, rather than slaves or soldiers. Hurry."

Across the City, looters did indeed provide an indelible mark. There were cries of women being violated, and property being destroyed.

Women, as always seemed to be an easy target. Yet at some of the churches and from the top of buildings and balconies, women pelted many of the scum with rocks and other elements that were easy to throw to cause damage.

One group held out as if their lives depended on it; Orhan, the Turkish prince. He knew what lay in wait if he surrendered. There would be no surrender as his contingent continued the fight. Having honed his skills in the years of his 'detention' in Constantinople, and knowing the bitter hatred that existed between the sultan and his bloodline, the resistance was fierce. Death would arrive with honour. Ironically, as the city was changing from a Christian to Muslim city, the last resistance was coming from fighters of the latter religion; a religion that was different to the one the emperor espoused and embraced with the Pope.

⋆⋆

Captain Michalis had suffered yet another injury. He was being tended to by a nurse, who doubled as a warrior. Unlike anyone else in his position, the captain was remaining firm at his post. His fighters had spread across three towers; choosing to fill any void presented by dead or departed foreign fighters.

The sun was now high in the sky and he could see the banner of the enemy flapping from a number of towers. He was not perturbed, after all, he was from Crete.

In his thick Cretan dialect, "we will destroy whoever attempts to take any tower."

Zaganos, who was in no mood to join the irregulars in their early round of looting, held the steady discipline of his men below the tower. He wanted the prize of Michalis' scalp. The Cretan did not let the local barber in Chania touch his scalp, and he was not about to allow a converted Commander from the Ottoman army touch his scalp.

As the day unfolded into hours, there were pockets of stiff resistance. Kantakouzenos, conscious that his ancestors had been too selfish to preserve the strength of Constantinople, kept fighting with his core group of Greek fighters, which included monks.

The Bocchiardi brothers were determined to imitate machines and intended to make up for the error of Kerkoporta. They fought on, occasionally surrounded; occasionally smashing their way through until one of the trio valiantly fell. The fighters, on their horses, had finally run out of options and dashed to the harbour.

The sultan had promised looting, which by custom allowed for killing soldiers and taking children as prisoners. The bothers witnessed and later learned that many sick and pathetic 'men' raped women and some of the children. Public buildings and churches were being desecrated, as they cantered along. There was nothing the Bocchiardi could do now.

Elsewhere, some of the small villages surrendered to Ottoman commanders, and were afforded protection for their obedience. This contrasted to the uncivil behaviour witnessed in most parts of Constantinople.

All foreigners made a play for the harbour. By and large, most safely escaped with the earlier departures.

For a fleeting moment though, this seemed tenuous to the captain of the Venetian fleet, who was convinced that Venice was sending a huge relief fleet consulted with the podesa of Galata. They discussed launching a counterattack; "otherwise dislodge that damn fucking chain along the wall of Galata and let all ships leave."

Despite the general disarray of the defenders, the Ottomans were no longer in organised units, intent on looting and damaging the city for personal gain. A counterattack would normally appeal to many of the Venetians, the emperor or the Bocchiardi brothers, however, there was no realistic chance it would have achieved much, save for greater misery. All the great warriors were either slain or accepting of the situation. Thus, the decision was made to allow the dislodgement of the chain in the Horn by the podesa. He was now completely aware that he would need to send a grovelling emissary to Mehmed, later that day to ask that Galata be spared, 'as a neutral city.'

⋆⋆

The Cretans were not fleeing. This was not what Cretans were about. Honour was their custom. Bravery was their nature.

"For the honour of our land, the emperor and God, we will not be beaten by the dogs." The words of the captain were met with foolhardy enthusiasm in what could only be described as a weary and hopeless situation.

As the lyra played in the background by one of the soldiers, the Cretans once again rained down a barrage of arrows, stones, spit and curses.

Zaganos knew the arrows would stop eventually and once more sent up a group of Janissaries to fight their way through. Despite the discipline and training of the Janissaries, they were no match for the wide-eyed Cretans. One by one, the enemy was mowed down with projectiles or hand to hand combat.

The Cretans were called dogs. Grudgingly.

⋆⋆

From a distance, the sultan stood back. Aware that he had promised three days of pillaging, he did not want to enter the conquered city, just yet. He was admiring the game of tavli that was unfolding in front of him.

"In another time, these pesky Cretans could be useful for me. Dare I say it, they are the equal of any fighter who has walked this earth," he thought to himself.

Zaganos rallied his troops and led the charge himself. The result did not change, as the bodies piled up. Frustrated, Zaganos was set to prepare a cannon in order to try blasting them out.

It was at that moment, an eagle landed in front of him. He looked up and saw a messenger from the sultan.

"My dear commander, I have conquered enough. I will show my clemency to a brave band of men who are a long way from their home, and I imagine, want to return where they will be welcomed. They will also take with them the stories of this siege and conquest, and some of my clemency," the message read.

"We should call Mehmed, the Conqueror. Note to thyself, propose this idea at the war council meeting," Zaganos thought.

"Offer them a safe passage with any vessels of their choosing with provisions. These Cretans have earned valour. They should be entitled to return to Crete, for there will come a time when I need to seek a new territory and will want to fight a tough adversary. Until then, our troops salute their bravery, and will fight them no more," ended the message.

Zaganos approached under a banner of truce and spoke to the captain. The captain acknowledged the Commander and the message.

⋆⋆

The Cretans, faced with the impossible task of holding out against thousands of men or returning home to safeguard Crete, decided to take the offer which allowed them to keep their weapons and most importantly, their lyra. These proud warriors had brought a new meaning to the term heroism and bravery throughout the campaign. A testament to what Byzantium had once stood for and what the Immortal Emperor had displayed in the frantic final moments of Greek rule over the city.

Chapter 36

Theodora

The crew didn't even pretend to be an Ottoman vessel. They knew they could outpace the Ottoman ships, as they were sailing through with a determined mind and a big heart. Theodora wanted to believe they could arrive in time. They had worked tirelessly to reach their destination; nothing, not even the Hisar or an iceberg would stop this determined lot.

The soldiers in the Hisar were always prepared for crazy Latin or Greek ships trying to force their way from the Black Sea. *Easy target,* they prepared.

⋆ ⋆

Taking a hit to the side was felt, as it rocked all on board. Yet, it was a minor hit, with minimal damage.

The wind was behind them as a flock of eagles came soaring through, skewering the sightline of the soldiers on the European shore. A few precious seconds. A few seconds that enabled them to avoid a second and fatal hit. Theodora was just a few kilometres from her love, the city and her emperor.

⋆ ⋆

The tendrils of smoke. Chaos. It was 6 am and the sun was still creeping above Constantinople. It kept revealing something that neither the crew nor Theodora had ever wanted to imagine or witness. Though there appeared to be sporadic fighting, the sultan's standard was flying over some of the towers.

It was a hopeless sight.

The quick-thinking Theodora changed the flag on the sails to the Ottoman standard and forced any of the crew who were crying to go below deck, lest they be found out.

"The situation is hopeless Theodora; not even God can help Constantinople now. If we dock we will end up as part of the pillaging and slave trade that will surely follow." An older Greek sailor who was steering, offered wise words.

Without a hint of anger or heartbreak, Theodora stared hard at the sight in front of her. "Let us follow those eagles to the Aegean, perhaps Lesvos. We can pick up any survivors who may be in the water or on the shores along the way." A tear finally slipped down her cheek. She looked away and over at the Asiatic side.

By the time her vessel had made its way past the danger, Theodora had picked up as many refugees as she could. The refugees had swam into the water to escape from the Ottomans. The upper deck was soon overflowing with wretched souls and a few scattered icons. A well-known thespian, who once rehearsed at the Hippodrome, stared longingly at the walls of the city. She gave Theodora a hug. "My name is Despoina. Thank you."

⋆⋆

As the barbarians rushed into the church, some with blood on them, swords drawn, and the faces that only a devil could appreciate, the priests called for calm. The chanting from the choir remained, as if the chanters were oblivious to the intruders.

This final sermon in Hagia Sophia was ready for a final twist. The priests turned to the congregation. "Do not be afraid my flock. You will all be martyrs and welcomed to the heaven above."

The barbarians were now focussed on the priests. The chanting continued unabated.

"We will end our sermon here. We will return one day with the immortal emperor to finish the sermon in our church. Pray for the redemption of the barbarians' souls, for they know no better."

The priests vanished into the wall. The barbarians chased, seemingly coming up against a brick wall. There was no secret door or sliding wall, the priests had vanished into thin air. The barbarian commander asked for a thorough search of the church. The priests could not be located. Just like the body of the apparent, fallen emperor.

"Ok forget the priests, let's finish these people and collect our bounty," said the barbarian, who was unable to understand the irony of trashing a peaceful house of God.

Chapter 37

Alternative ending, what very nearly happened, or did it. . . .

The ranking officers called on the rag tag of bashi-bazouk men to head for the walls first. Or rather head to a certain slaughter. The Ottoman leaders had little love for this group. They were depending on looting as their main inspiration to climb those walls, were lightly armed. They were truly a composite group of men.

Barbaro, the doctor on duty at Romanus, made a point to note when he compiled his own chronicles. “Muslims, Barbarians, Germans, other Christians. What a strange group, with a mixture of bows, scimitars, spears and many greedy eyes.”

For the sultan, these may have been a motley bunch, but they were there to sap the energy of the defenders. A clever strategy indeed. Before breaking for attacking positions a few hours earlier, Zaganos had instructed them to charge at a decent pace when the time would come. The ditches in front of them had, by now, been filled in the weeks of fighting and were easy to cross over. Some of

Figure 37.1: Constant siege. Image courtesy of Steve Estvanik.

the irregulars prepared to use their arrows, while others brought wooden ladders for the walls.

"How do they not realise that wooden ladders will be burnt if we choose that course of action?" It was the Catalan leader, voicing his approval of their stupidity to his friend the emperor.

The emperor simply shook his head and shrugged. "That is why they are fighting us rather than standing tall on our side of these walls. Surely, they are missing brains and hearts."

⋆⋆

The emperor now stepped forward. With his height, charisma, royal outfit and sword in his hand, he looked every inch imperial and ready to lead.

He had spent the last hour riding to key points on the wall to urge the defenders on.

"Men, women, citizens, friends. This is our last stand. Tonight, we will rise one more time and defeat the infidel. They call us dogs, yet we are not the ones running on four legs to steal a city that does not belong to them. We have come this far. Together, for we are all in this together, we will fight one more time. I will see you again for a victory celebration. May God be with you."

Despite the horns and trumpets that musically climbed the walls, the defenders all cheered. Some broke out into church hymns and chanting.

At 1.40 am, the emperor addressed troops at Romanus Gate, reminding all and sundry the honour they will now bring to themselves, "for no defenders in the history of warfare have stood as firm, tenacious and proud as you have. We have withstood them for weeks, heroically.

Giustiniani waited until the emperor had finished his rousing speech and the cheering had slowed. Surveying the ladders and the resources he had, he simply demanded that the ladders be pushed back. One by one, a poorly thought out attack; ladders falling, and the enemy being crushed on the piles of debris over the ditches in front of the outer wall.

Some of the more ingenuous attackers were able to use ropes to affix ladders. They were being shielded by a fierce volley of arrows emanating from the rear. This time, the second group of irregulars seemed to be making an impact.

Across the way, the sultan looked on, waiting for the next move from Giustiniani.

The Genoan simply called for Greek fire and oil to be spread across the wall. One by one, the ladders with ropes were burnt to ash.

More waves came to the wall. Cannons also blasted overhead. The defenders were not wavering.

"We have lost many fighters, Constantine. I am calling in the reserve 300 to join us in the next hour as I can see more losses coming."

The emperor nodded and took up his position to the left of Romanus. It was not unusual to see the emperor provide instructions, encourage people or talk tactics with the Genoan. Those around him could be seen ducking and weaving stray arrows. The emperor had no such compunction. He felt that only Achilles could be struck from a stray arrow, and Achilles he was not. The beard and the difference in costume being some of the distinguishers.

Irregulars kept at it for two hours. Occasionally, a few made it to the top of the wall where they were met by skilled fighters. Dead bodies of the enemy suddenly became the biggest impediment as the enemy losses piled up.

The emperor ordered nonfighting citizens such as monks and nuns to dump the bodies back over the walls. It was a contrasting image, people of God disposing bodies while behind them the occasional attacker who had made it over the wall was being brought down by swords, meeting a violent and unholy fate. A monk had to duck as a crazy attacker attempted to chop off his head as a souvenir for visiting Constantinople. Fortunately, the emperor was a few metres away, with a spear he had just picked up, and threw it accurately before the attacker could try his luck again.

Many irregulars had become irritated at the way the attack was playing out and tried to return to camp. Commanders had anticipated the move and deployed elite soldiers with whips and swords to force them back to their certain death.

In this way, a sea of bodies would tell the story of thousands of dead. This would be a perfect end for the campaign if only the Mehmed could take a hint and call it off.

Instead, he kept urging the fleet in the Horn to continue bombarding the walls as a demonstration of power, while preparing for the second phase attack at Romanus.

After 3.30 am, the second assault was signalled. Cannon balls blasting as the second phase troops were being inspired by the Sultan.

"For the glory of your Anatolian lands. For the glory of your Sultan. You have history calling. These infidel are ready to be defeated. Go my good men, my friends, and take us to Constantinople, which is promised."

The second wave consisted of better trained soldiers with stronger armour, significant military experience and a love for their Sultan rather than just merely looting. They marched in military precision, disciplined and with the learnings of the failed first attack as a guide for their actions. They also possessed more courage, against a tired defence.

"Why don't you send us back the other lot?" It was Grant lamenting how this was not a fair fight. Fresh fighters against exhausted spirits.

Unusual for this time of night, a number of eagles flew past the inner walls.

⋆⋆

Giustiniani, was just like the emperor. He understood how to lead and motivate from the front line. There was no amount of convincing these two warriors, they would not budge from their positions on the front line.

Down below, Zaganos knew that if you cut off the head of the lion, it may deter the rest of the beasts. He had instructed the commanders at the earlier pre-war briefing to try hard to scale the point where emperor and the Genoan would meet every few minutes.

⋆⋆

The Anatolian soldiers with shields and determination were ironically not shielded well enough. A flood of arrows, rocks and small cannon balls smashed most of the front line. A monk even threw his cross which hit one soldier on the back of his head, killing him instantly.

The sultan, certainly someone with genius and smarts, was wise enough to avoid the frontline. Instead, shouting enthusiastically loud for his men to feel inspired.

Grant, yet again leant next to the person beside him and asked, "why doesn't he show the bravery of the emperor and lead the charging forces? I know he isn't that slim but surely he can canter slowly behind the front line or soldiers; or should I say, frontline corpses?"

The Anatolian regiments pushed on. Some reaching the walls before meeting their makers shortly after. Others used climbing equipment and ladders to generate an impression, before they too met their maker.

As the defenders had gained the edge, the Anatolian troops retreated to regroup. This temporary pause was fortuitous, for the gun of Orban, who had long since met his maker, delivered a form of redemption. A large ball smashed a hole; an invitation for the Anatolians to return with a sense of vengeance and purpose as smoke, the darkness of the evening and yelling created a vertigo moment for the defenders. The attackers came thick and fast.

"Giustiniani, we need the hole patched," came frantic shouting.

"Giustiniani we need to retreat," came a voice from the Latins.

The experienced Giustiniani knew exactly how to respond.

"Shortly, a few of their men will come through that hole. There is no need to panic. Carrying their shields, swords and body armour will tire them. Allow them to pour into the gap between the inner and outer wall. Francisco take 20 of your finest Catalonians and stand with your backs to the inner wall. They will come at you. My troops, I need you to spread across the outer wall. When they come through the courtyard, as it is narrow, jump down and encircle them."

Continuing, "Greeks, I want a dozen of you on either side of the breach, at a distance. Let their first men pass. Then fire down every missile you can. Citizens, you have the toughest task. With the help of God, try to patch up that stupid hole. No one likes a hole like that. It looks unbecoming on such a beautiful wall."

The orders were obeyed with expediency. The Anatolians, incredulous at their success had a *what now*? moment and simply poured into the gap between inner and outer. 200 of them to be precise. Ready to take on the Catalan and the Genoans. Rushing toward them in a *rope a dope* moment, Toledo did not budge. The leader of the charging contingent did not understand why until it was too late. Venetians, Genoans, Greeks and the Varangian Guards quickly encircled all of the invaders. One by one in quick succession, they were hacked, stabbed, slashed and smashed. Not a soul survived. The emperor cheered from above and returned to martialling the wall.

⋆⋆

Elsewhere, Halil had tried another invasion from the Marmara, which was equally unsuccessful, though, the sultan had expected that; having also lost faith in Halil to push as hard as possible. "I will deal with him when the time comes," he had confided in Zaganos.

In the Horn, the bombardment from the ships there continued, though they were similarly unable to make a breach. This area proved a real humiliation as it was defended by a mixture of monks, Greeks and Turks, men and some women. The Horn had proven to be a friend, as the conditions in the water had been far from steady for what would normally be a good seafaring time of the year.

At the Blachernae Palace end, the Bocchiardi Brothers were as defiant as ever. Certainly Paolo, Troilo and Antonio, all the o's were not the type to take a backward step, and they were joined by Geronimo and Leonardo di Langasco, also brothers, and a few more of their Genoan friends. Between cursing the attackers and making fun of them, all the brothers seemingly enjoyed siege warfare. There was nothing that could shake these Venetians who fought under the flag of St Mark. The emperor had joined in, with a quip, the previous evening, "if I notice just a scratch on my palace behind you, I will hold you to account and withdraw you from further siege duties." The brothers laughed; it is claimed that the laughter may have caused one of the brothers to break a rib!

A frustrated leader of the Ottomans was now at his wit's end as runners kept delivering messages that no attack had succeeded at any of the points around the walls. One of his runners had the guile to report that the Bocchiardi brothers had even made a counterattack. Coming out of a locked gate, savaging dozens of the enemy.

The poor showing of the Anatolians against the brave defenders ensured that thousands more had fallen, to add to the irregulars' list of fatalities. If points were given for body count, it is clear who the victor was. Four hours of fighting had come to this. He turned 180 degrees to see the Janissaries, lancers, personal bodyguards and the last of his elite forces. Over 5,000 ready to attack the weakest part of the wall. All told, there were now less than 7,000 exhausted soldiers spread across the entire length of the city remaining. This number was topped up with monks, nuns, foreigners and citizens. Joining them, were church bells and those who were reciting prayers at some of the churches.

⋆⋆

The sultan gave the order. There was no time for he did not wish the enemy to recoup any energy with a respite. This was his last throw of the dice. His elite forces and Janissaries would outnumber the enemy five to one at Romanus. They were good odds for someone like Grant, should he have wished to create a bet spread.

Grant, this time, was focussed on one element. To avenge his wife's death by chopping down as many of the bastard enemy as he could. His eyes were wide eyed and his heart racing. Just like most of the defenders. Other moments, he was salivating and at others he was red with anger. "Come on you damn enemy, is that the best you have?" He shouted with fury at the attackers.

⋆⋆

Their elites were led by a range of disciplined heavy infantry. The sultan leading the way as far as the ditch in front of Romanus. Would the name of a disgraced emperor from a bygone era have yet another negative impact on the empire, or will there be redemption?

Mehmed ordered for a constant battery of archers, cannon, spears and any other projectile to land over the wall, taking out as many defenders as possible in the process. Under this cover, the elites made their dash. Many succeeded in attaching ladders, others used barrels that were hanging on the walls from the previous Greek fire torrents. The defenders tried to shower these attackers with rocks, javelins and dead bodies. The first *wave* was supressed. The second followed, and soon more. The defenders would have preferred waves in the ocean to waves of potential death. Eventually, a good number made it on to the rampart with fierce and ferocious fighting taking place. Again, the defenders could claim the victory, only this time, a few of the defenders were also part of the casualties.

Both Giustiniani and the emperor repulsed attackers, with the nobility joining Constantine to eliminate a good number. Lifelong training and vigilance had steeled these fighters for such encounters.

The emperor was always in his element when he could use his sword.

The cardinal looked on proudly, knowing that victory was here and soon the Pope would send reinforcements to Constantinople. Along with the reunification of the churches, he felt his work for God had been complete.

⋆ ⋆

"There is always a moment for a laugh and high confidence. There are moments like these when focus and conservative instincts should take place," Lukas told me, as we stood a few hundred metres from the Blachernae Palace, he observed and responded to the carelessness of the brothers and their men. One of them, tasked with locking the gate behind them when returning from a daring attack, had failed to lock the gate behind them. Perhaps a moment of fatigue? Stupidity? It mattered not as a band of Ottomans snuck in. They quickly tore down the flags of the empire and the standard of St Mark and replaced them with the sultan's, providing the attackers outside with a glimmer of hope.

Lukas sent troops to help the brothers and their men; having been surprised, they were struggling to hold these determined intruders from inching further. The intruders were surrounded by this relief force, however, the loss of fighters was significant, contrasting with the morale boost to the outside invaders.

⋆⋆

Back at the Romanus Gate, the elites of the sultan had been defeated. Just a few more were willing to chance their luck against the crazy defenders.

The sultan was preparing to decide. The moment of retreat was running through his head. Tens of thousands of soldiers had perished in the campaign with almost half on this day alone.

An Ottoman archer of merit, who would have been a noble entry to the ancient Greek Games, was able to take a shot. A shot that he had been wanting to undertake for the last hour. "Take out the leader of the lions and you have an advantage, if not a decisive one," he thought.

He could see the tall, bearded target, leading the troops. The archer could see how they listened, a man of honour and charisma. With one eye closed and the other focussed, he shot the arrow.

It missed. The eagle above him proved to be a distraction.

The sultan looked around. Having now listened to more news from his runners. The stars were fading. The sun was being readied from a restless evening of sleep.

The archer took aim one last time. It flew through the air, on an upward trajectory. It may have skimmed the tip of the wall and somehow it landed. The landing was through a gap in the armour of the Genoan. Who shot the arrow? I will never be sure.

⋆⋆

A buzz of drama and excitement ensued. Giustiniani took a step forward and collapsed. Immediately he was rushed by some of his men. Barbaro was summonsed to help the fallen hero.

"Can you take me to my ship for treatment? I do not wish to be treated up here as a distraction and if the enemy breach the line again. . . ."

Barbaro declined. "I think it wise you remain here." The Genoans therefore called for another medical practitioner, someone not aligned with Venice who could meet Giustiniani at his boat in the boom of the Horn.

The emperor was informed and told that the Genoan will be taken to his ship.

The emperor, without hesitation rushed to see the Genoan, who was bleeding and bruised at the point of penetration.

"How are you feeling? Status?"

Starting to feel the injury through the shock, the Genoan replied, "I need to get proper treatment. The medicine and tools we need are on my ship. The soldiers will hold the line."

The emperor was too experienced and seasoned enough to understand, any retreat of the Genoan would give the attackers hope.

The Janissaries were scouring the wall searching for any visual of the fallen Genoan. The leader of the Ottomans was now informed of the situation.

"Commander, friend, please stay at your post. I beg of you with all my life, do not abandon us, not now." Came an impassioned plea from the emperor. "You are not a coward; you need to stay with us."

"I will return, you have my word. I just need to get the treatment."

A horrified emperor reluctantly allowed the struggling body of the Genoan, to be stretchered away.

Despite the advantage held by the defenders, dozens of his troops followed their leader, like a puppy following their master.

Except this was not a moment to play fetch. Victory was just there, and Giustiniani was there too. Then gone. This mini panic was soon exacerbated by more of his troops who thought their leader was fleeing Constantinople, rather than understanding the seriousness of the injury meant treatment on his boat was the best option.

Dissent broke out between some of the Greeks and the Genoan's troops. In this ill-advised moment for debate, the sultan ordered yet another 'final' surge.

"Allah Akbar" could be heard repeatedly, deafening.

The emperor rallied the Greeks and any of the remaining Genoans. An already tired and steadily depleted section on the ramparts would now need to find a strength that bellied their numbers. Outside, all available troops of every class made their way forward. This time, the Greek Fire was limited owing to lack of numbers and chemical ingredients.

Hasan Ulubatlı, a formidable member of the cavalry managed to climb the wall with a group of 30. He was just a few years older than his sultan. He had a sword, shield and the banner of the sultan. He was promised *immortality* should he become the first person who could fly the flag of his empire. Clearly, the earlier achievement at the Blachernae palace walls had been forgotten by the enemy as the sultan cheered and urged on Hasan from a distance. "Plant our banner, be the first," could be heard.

The Greeks fought the group of 30 who proved no match for the ever-alert defenders. Hasan, however, held on to the banner, inspiring the thousands who were now throwing themselves into battle one last time. If Hasan can hold onto the banner, if others join him and raise flags, it will surely be the turning point for the sultan.

The emperor was having none of it. He brushed off a pesky, would-be attacker by simply throwing him off the wall.

"Damn, that must have hurt," he thought to himself.

Constantine ran like a man possessed; his double headed emblazoned eagle on his sword ready to soar just like the eagles above in the sky. He struck the banner, before another blow was received to the carrying hand of Hasan.

The banner dropped, as the sultan looked up from a distance.

Hasan dropped his shield and used his right hand to hold his sword to meet the next vengeful blow of the emperor.

The Greeks fought the group of 30, who proved no match. All of the Hellenic blades seem to hit their targets, finding ways to penetrate body armour. Shields were useless against the speed of the Greeks. Tired they were, their speed did not let up as they danced and weaved around their enemy. Italian sandals and boots may have also made a slight difference when moving around swiftly. Hasan, however, held his own against the purple robed fighter. A fierce dual continued, each time the emperor met the blade of Hasan, Hasan defended and retaliated. It was quick and fierce. Neither fighter willing to concede.

It went back and forth. Hasan swung and just managed to pierce the chain mail of his adversary. No wound is going to stop the emperor. As the now confident Hasan attempted a follow up blow, the emperor threw his blade from one hand to the other, turned 360 degrees and drove his imperial sword under the uncovered part of Hasan's neck, who stepped a few paces forward before falling forward, head-first into the ground.

"Now that was one tough fighter."

The emperor turned to see who had spoken in a *foreign accented* Greek language, that was filled with pain in the speaker's voice. It was Giustiniani, clutching two of his men. Sweating, bleeding from his bandages and pale white.

"If I am to die, let it be in full view of these dogs. We fight to the end."

Constantine hugged his friend. The meaning of the moment was not lost on him.

The Genoan men who had fled as if in a hurry to gain the closing market specials had returned to their defensive positions. Just in time, just. For hundreds more of the enemy were seeking the same glory that Hasan sought. Carrying flags and banners. One by one they were either rounded up and slaughtered or shot down with a hail of arrows or fire. Giustiniani had the citizens bring back a fresh supply of arrows and ingredients for the Greek fire.

At the peak of penetrating attackers, just after Hasan had bravely fallen, there may have been over a thousand attackers all at once on the outer walls. Few had spilled into the gap between the inner and outer walls, unless they had concluded their duties on earth. Dozens of the defenders were valiantly fighting from the walls, with projectiles, barrels, swords and Greek Fire. Dozens more were bringing projectiles to these soldiers or arrows to the archers. The tight space was packed like a feast or fiesta for a saint, except rather than some dancing and drinking wine, it was hand to hand combat with equally marched armour and weaponry.

The archers from the pope, were now a blessing as they picked off some of the Ottomans from the tower above.

Ultimately, the notion that anything less a victory will keep them alive, spurred the defenders. Fighting with a spirit that belied their fatigue.

⋆⋆

Conjuring up the spirit of heroes of Greece and Rome, they used their knowledge and experience of fighting on the walls to gain the upper hand. The emperor was an easy target for would be attackers, but his superior fighting skills and ability to step around and plunge a sword into his enemy was almost unparalleled. His renewed energy may have been down to the sight of his Genoan friend re-appearing. A mortally wounded Giustiniani remained in a far corner protected by his men. His presence was enough. His time on earth was expiring as his eyes fought off the shutdown. He was going nowhere this time, save for a more peaceful place.

A good twenty minutes of hard fighting had whittled the enemy down to 20 percent of the volume seen before. The walls were soaked with blood, fallen soldiers and dropped daggers and swords.

One last hope remained for the enemy. On the order of a commander, they all tried to rush the emperor in a do or die stand. Now the emperor may be one tough individual against any other individual or two, but a few dozen would make it difficult, for he was not Hercules or Sampson despite his long locks.

"For glory, for the sultan," came a hair-splitting cry, and many of the Greeks were actually full of chest and head hair. As two would be assassins lunged at the emperor while he was holding off a further two, Grant dropped his sword and dived in front of Constantine.

The emperor could not believe the courage of the Scotsman, who quickly fell to the ground as a hail of arrows met his assassins.

The nobility quickly stepped in front of the emperor and the common people. It was their moment to truly earn their birthright as they held off the remaining attackers.

The ferocious battle continued. Up stepped Toledo and the emperor to join the nobility. Francisco himself was a member of the Spanish nobility, oddly having volunteered to make his way to defend a fellow Christian noble, he was accepted by the Catalonians to lead them; some would say owing to his dashing finely cut black outfits presented him as a real elite, which he changed on a daily basis. The nobility of Constantinople had been happy to have him, as one of the few who came to protect Christendom.

Sticking to a narrow confine, they were able to hold off the attackers, while to their sides the Greeks held off any attackers. Blood, bodies, yelling, screaming and the clanking of steel could be heard.

An eagle swooped down just as one would be attacker tried to fell the emperor, distracting the assailant.

A spear managed to hit the emperor, piercing the edge of his gold breast plate. He simply pulled it out, boomeranging it back, killing a stunned Janissary.

The hand to hand fighting continuing for a further nine minutes. The weight of numbers in the narrow confines favoured the emperor as well as the skill and standard of the defending fighters. They were amongst the best in the world. The Catalan leader, trained in the art of grappling and Bull Fighting was now in a position to throw any remaining adversaries over the wall. Remember, if you piss him off, you simply awaken a deep dark nature that lurks beneath his good-natured surface.

It was just a matter of time. The sultan had to make a decision to leave.

Instead, he prepared yet another 'final' wave. The death count meant little. He had the reserves, but he was shaken. If he could not win this next attempt, it would surely be over.

The sun was up, a blinding distraction just after the eagles had flown past, yet in the Bosporus they could see something growing larger by the second. It was a pirate ship flying the imperial flag and the flag of St Mark. Theodora was on her way. *Perhaps Trebizond was on its way.*

Down by the Marmara, 17 ships could now be seen in the distance. Was this an advance force from Venice?

Hilal spoke to the sultan in his usual measured and mature tone. "It is over for now. If Trebizond has sent down some ships and Venice is advancing with a relief force, likely a hundred ships, it will mean Galata joins the circus; and we cannot trust the Serbs. We have inflicted enough damage. We are the victors no matter what. Financially they are ruined and will never recover."

He knew what he would do with Hilal when he returned to

Adrianople. Reluctantly, he gave the order to raise the siege. The depleted military quickly retreated, with an escort of eagles hovering above. They too were tired. In the background along the now empty spaces, dogs of all breeds and colours were lying next to each other in comfort and peace. There are no dogs here.

Chapter 38

Postscript

Immediately after the conquest, church bells, altars, icons, and relics were removed from Hagia Sofia. The holy frescoes and mosaics depicting Jesus, his mother Mary, Christian saints, and angels were eventually destroyed or plastered over. The church was known throughout the world, a symbol of triumph for the Greek Orthodox and the Byzantines, a visual wonder for all those who visited.

Mehmed, despite having promised the customary three days of pillage to his military, decided to enter the city after allowing the Cretans safe passage out of Constantinople. He was appalled by the destruction and ordered that the pillaging must end by sundown. Fortunately, there was no day light savings to prolong the misery of the defeated. He was particularly annoyed to see public buildings attacked.

Making his way to Hagia Sofia, he knelt down in front of the great church, taking dirt off the ground and sprinkling that over his turban in a sign of humility. He entered to see the vandalism and took a *shining* to one such soldier who was breaking off parts of the altar. He beat the soldier to his near death for his greed and

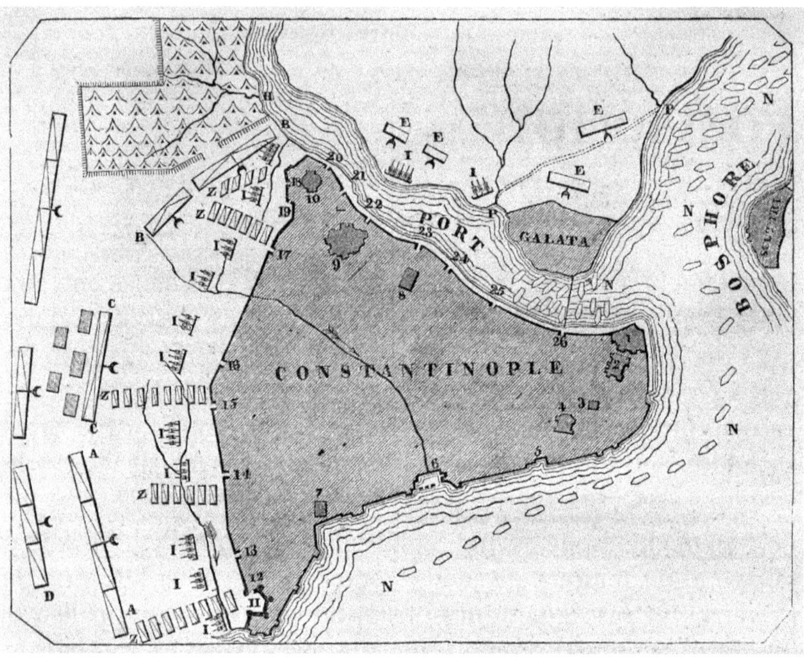

Figure 38.1: Constantinople map. Image courtesy of Marzolino.

then ordered that the church be converted to a mosque immediately. Such was his impression of what he saw.

Despite 30,000 people being sold as slaves, he eventually encouraged/brought back Christians to help repopulate Constantinople. Most of whom were Greek, ensuring a large percentage of the population of Constantinople remained Greek, until the senseless elimination of Greeks, Armenians and Assyrians during the twentieth century. Greeks had mostly lived with Turks, Jews, Kurds and Arabs peacefully since 1453. At the time of writing, there are less than 5,000 in the city. The great church, having been converted to a museum in 1934 (a decent compromise), is once again a mosque, thanks to the anti-secular policies of the president.

Some of the protagonists of the siege managed to survive. Yet again cardinal Isodore was able to escape from a dangerous scenario; dressed as a commoner, having exchanged clothes with a dead man in the street. His heroic deeds were never forgotten in Rome when he returned. Notaras, survived briefly before being executed as he was not willing to give up his children.

Another who was unable to survive the chop was Grand Vizier, Hilal Pasha. He was summoned to the sultan and summarily executed. Not even amnesia would allow him to forget his sympathy toward the emperor.

Gennadius Scholarius was elevated to the role of patriarch of the church on the condition he immediately renounce the union with the Vatican; a bittersweet victory for him. He ensured key buildings and churches were spared from the looting, providing an advance force of guards to protect infrastructure he deemed essential to the running of the city. This included the Church of the Holy Apostles, which was set aside for the Gennadius, though it was demolished in 1461. This was the second biggest church in Constantinople, dating back to the reign of the first Constantine.

On the first of June, the new ruler of the city provided the symbolic signs including a mantle to the new patriarch, followed by a ceremony. This would become the tradition between sultan and patriarch, the latter would evolve to become the leader of the millet (Christian nation) system, a system that was fully in place by the following century. The Greeks would belong to the Rum millet.

Gennadius was well known as an anti-unionist, the main criteria for Mehmed to appoint him. During the siege, he posted a note on his door to his fellow Greeks wondering why they put their faith in the Italians rather than trusting God. “In losing your faith you will lose your city.” It was ironic, for he was originally a pro unionist who attended a unionist Council of Florence in 1440 where he delivered a series of speeches in favour of unionism.

Over the next few years, the sultan mopped up the remaining Greek territories of the Byzantine Empire, including the Morea, any outlying pockets in Thrace and the Trebizond Empire in 1461. The Principality of Theodoro survived until 1475.

The victory of the sultan, albeit by the skin of his teeth, created his status as the Conqueror. In modern Turkey, he is rightfully revered, perhaps second only to the Thessaloniki-born Kemal Ataturk, for his deeds and victories.

Mehmed set the platform for the empire to continue expanding. This was only checked by the battle of Vienna in 1663.

The Ottomans would become one of the largest empires in history thanks to Mehmed. Similar to the Byzantines in the past, they held North Africa, the Near East including Syria, a good chunk of the Black Sea, the Balkans; they also managed a foray into Italy at the old Greek city of Otranto in 1580, which was held for 14 months. It is interesting to note that 800 male captives were offered the chance to live if they converted. Led by a textile worker who encouraged his fellow citizens to choose death, the entire group of captives chose death! Otranto, resulted in a fightback supported by the pope, as well as France, Hungary and other European territories.

The pope, like all leaders across Europe, was heartbroken about the loss of Constantinople. He urged a new crusade. Despite the tears shed by Frederick in Germany, there was no great push for a crusade. Only the fearsome Vlad the Impaler was willing to lead a crusade in 1459, though without Europe wide support, it went nowhere fast.

If many of the Europeans had dispatched well-organised and disciplined troops, cavalry, ships and supplies, along with other regions, Constantinople would have held as a coalition. Add in the Russians and any other enemies of the Ottoman Empire, including the Turkish Karamanid Empire in Asia Minor, Trebizond, Georgia, Hungary, Serbia and Greece proper, Constantinople would have survived. In turn, the sultan's hold on his own empire would have weakened. Ironically, the Serbs and Greeks would one day unite for the Balkan Wars of 1912-13 to defeat the Ottomans and then Bulgaria.

Late Byzantium had provided poets, writers, humanists, performers, architects, philosophers, musicians and artists, complemented by theologians for centuries. Many had made their way to Italy, especially Venice which became a hub for Greeks, for learning and for the renaissance.

History is filled with losers. In Constantinople, the people were essentially the real losers. They had not invited the Ottomans to take their city, or their great church. The majority of these brave people were killed, beaten, enslaved and/or raped. Winners in history have tended to do the same, usually to serve as a warning to others in the future. It does not matter if they believe in a higher power, human beings have an ability to let barbarism come into play. For every Martin Luther King and Sojourner Truth, there is an evil lurking to come to the fore. From ancient times until now, the only difference is that barbarity has decreased slightly since WW2. We still have a long way to go though.

For centuries, Greeks believed that the emperor was taken by some sort of angel and turned into marble. He now *resides* in a cave under the Golden Gate, which is where the emperors entered the city in triumph after successful campaigns. Anyway, it is believed that the emperor will one day return to rule Constantinople. How he would fare in this day and age of equality, social media, e-commerce and football as the true global language/religion is something I would be very keen to witness!

Despite the general massacre and pillage that took place as soon as the city was captured, it must be said that the Conqueror, like most of those who would rule from Constantinople, was pragmatic and sought to rule a harmonious and multi-ethnic empire. Until the late 1700s, the Ottomans were mainly gracious rulers, allowing freedom of worship. The Greek community grew strong economically and despite paying high taxes and occasionally providing young boys for the Janissary regimen (this was the highly trained military unit, disturbingly made up of former Christian boys that were forcibly converted to Islam), they enjoyed special privileges in the Ottoman Empire, which included running the bureaucracy and commerce in Constantinople, and elsewhere.

Thus by the turn of the 19th Century, the Greek population of Constantinople numbered approximately 200,000 people and of course Asia Minor had a population of two million Greeks. Unfortunately, as the Ottoman Empire declined, the graciousness of the hosts declined. More and more Church and Greek properties were confiscated by the authorities, a prelude to Turkish policies in the twentieth century and Greeks and other non-Turks were dealt with harshly. Inevitably, the rise of nationalism alongside the decline of the Ottoman Empire precipitated massacres and death marches of non-Turks. This was a disturbing way for the great and mainly tolerant empire to finish. I urge you to read up on this significantly tragic period, if you wish to know more.

By 1920, the city had a large population of 1.2 million people and was still known as Constantinople. Several years later, Kemal

Ataturk, the first leader and statesman of the new nationalist Turkish, would change the name to Istanbul. The name is a play on the Greek term, "I stin polis," which means "to the city."

The incredibly sad population exchange between Greece and Turkey in 1923 after the disastrous Asia Minor catastrophe (1.1 million Greeks from mainland Turkey and 380,000 Turks from Greece), ensured relative calm had begun to ensue by the early 1930s. In fact, Eleftherios Venizelos, the Greek statesman, had nominated Kemal Ataturk for a Nobel peace prize, much to the bewilderment of the organisers and Greeks in general.

With the goal of a nationalist Turkey complete, Ataturk promoted tolerance and secularism which was of great comfort to the Greeks living in Constantinople and the islands of strategic importance near Turkey of Imvros and Tenedos, as well as for the Muslims in the Greek state of Thrace. Both these areas were excluded from the population exchange between Turkey and Greece under the terms of agreement of the Treaty of Lausanne, signed by the two countries in 1923.

It is a reasonable assessment to make that despite the turbulent history, Greeks and Turks in Constantinople lived relatively harmoniously in the years after the signing of the Treaty of Lausanne. It took the issue of Cyprus to shatter this illusion and by 1955, the tensions between the Greek state and Turkey over Cyprus had become intolerable.

A pogrom and anti-Greek practises led to a decline of Greeks in Constantinople and Imvros and Tenedos. This is a tragedy, when you consider just how closely linked the cultures of these two peoples are, as the Byzantine and Ottoman entities overlapped each other, and many towns were shared by Christian and Muslim people; usually people tolerated each other in peace. It is little wonder that when the pettiness of politics is not in the equation, there are essentially few problems. I myself enjoy visiting Turkey and having worked with numerous Turkish people in a Turkish dominated suburb. It is easy to see many similarities and how rich the cultures of the Greeks and Turks are. Warm and hospitable people.

Ecumenical Patriarch Bartholomeus, leads the people from Constantinople and the Greek areas are noticeable. You can visit Hagia Sophia, a number of Greek Orthodox churches, the old fortifications of Constantinople and the Hippodrome.

There are a number of Greek schools in existence with approximately 260 pupils across all grades made up of Greek and Arab Christians. Greeks can be located in the modern areas of Nisantasi, Sisli, Kadikoy, Heybeliada (the headquarters of the Greek Orthodox Church), Buyukada, Burgaz, Yenikoy, Arnavuza, Kuzguncuk, Hatay and Adaraz, or the old areas of Kumkapi, Karagumruk, Samatya and Balat. In 2006, a conference on the future the Greek population of Turkey was held in Istanbul with the intention of finding real solutions to the problems encountered by those people and promoting a good relationship with the Turkish Government.

The pope's 2006, visit to the patriarch resulted in a very symbolic announcement that the old "Schism" between churches is now officially over. The two met again in 2015 on Lesvos during the refugee crisis.

In the same way that this millennium old feud between the Greek Orthodox of Constantinople and the Catholics of Rome is over, it is hoped that the feuds between Greeks and Turkish people also belong to the past. It is best to support a friendship and the ability of the two countries to continue down the path of peace and mutual respect. We are neighbours and we are people. Both believe in a God who is merciful.

Figure 38.2: Hagia Sophia. Image courtesy of *CC Graphics*.

About author

Billy Kotsis was born in Sydney to parents from the island of Lesvos, in 1977. Having spent almost a year of his childhood in Greece.

Upon entering university in 1995, he joined the well-organised and active Greek club, Macquarie University Greek Association. He spent four years learning about his own culture before making his way to Greece, again, in 1999. The love affair with Greece was *instant*. From that time onward he has spent most of his spare time researching his own Greek roots from Asia Minor and Lesvos as well as becoming fascinated with the remnants of Greek settlements in countries outside of Greece.

At last count, he had made his way to almost 60 countries and 80 Greek nisia.

A prolific writer, with over 250 of his articles appearing in Greek media in various countries.

Since 2012, he has written 17 short film and documentary projects, contributes to a blog, which features all of his history articles and has written or been involved with six book titles.

Despite his ancestry and having lost ancestors in Asia Minor, he holds no ill will toward Turkish people, seeking the path of friendship and peace.

Book titles

When Aussie Music Roared 2021

1453: Constantinople & the Immortal Rulers or there are no dogs here 2020

Once upon a time in Crystal Palace, Heart, football and life under Brexit: a fiction told by a Greek Aussie 2019

Fairwater Foodies Cookbook, Frasers Property Australia, editor/coordinator, contributor 2018

From Pyrrhus to Cyprus Forgotten and Remembered Hellenic Kingdoms, Territories, Entities & a Fiefdom 2017

The Many Faces of Hellenic Culture 2016

Most of these can be found on Amazon or the Greek Bilingual Bookshop.

Filmography

Tekno 2021

Magna Graecia: a visit to the Greko of Reggio 2021

Fabio's Tale of Olives 2020

Magna Graecia: the Greko of Calabria 2020

GRASSROOTS 2019

Magna Graecia: the Griko of Apulia 2019

An Olive Tale I&II: a journey through Italy and Greece 2019

An Olive Tale in Apulia short film 2018

Mykonos: the other side 2018

Bromance: Zorba gets a Girlfriend 2016

Lesvos: fall in Love 2015

The Draconian Decision of the German Drachma 1 2015

The Draconian Decision of the German Drachma 2 2014

Brutus vs Caesar: Winner takes London 2014

Leadership 2014

Zorba goes to Sydney 2013

YouTube Channel Billy Wood

Hellenic Travels to the Past www.herculean.wordpress.com

Contact executiveproducer@billywoodmovies.com

www.ingramcontent.com/pod-product-compliance
Ingram Content Group UK Ltd.
Pitfield, Milton Keynes, MK11 3LW, UK
UKHW020144250726
13967UKWH00002B/846

9 781513 665894